BOOKER'S MISSION

BROTHERHOOD PROTECTORS WORLD

TEAM EAGLE
BOOK ONE

KRIS NORRIS

Twisted Page Press LLC

To my cohorts... Jen, Delilah, Lori, and Kendall. Here's to a fantastic future.

And to all my fellow helicopter pilots.
I realize Booker's a bit larger-than-life, and I might have taken a few liberties, but no one reached the stars by staying grounded.

BROTHERHOOD PROTECTORS

ORIGINAL SERIES BY ELLE JAMES

Brotherhood Protectors Series

Montana SEAL (#1)

Bride Protector SEAL (#2)

Montana D-Force (#3)

Cowboy D-Force (#4)

Montana Ranger (#5)

Montana Dog Soldier (#6)

Montana SEAL Daddy (#7)

Montana Ranger's Wedding Vow (#8)

Montana SEAL Undercover Daddy (#9)

Cape Cod SEAL Rescue (#10)

Montana SEAL Friendly Fire (#11)

Montana SEAL's Mail-Order Bride (#12)

SEAL Justice (#13)

Ranger Creed (#14)

Delta Force Rescue (#15)

Dog Days of Christmas (#16)

Montana Rescue (#17)

Montana Ranger Returns (#18)

BROTHERHOOD PROTECTORS WORLD

ORIGINAL SERIES BY ELLE JAMES

Brotherhood Protectors Colorado World
Team EAGLE

Booker's Mission - Kris Norris
Hunter's Mission - Kendall Talbot
Gunn's Mission - Delilah Devlin
Xavier's Mission - Lori Matthews
Wyatt's Mission - Jen Talty

Team Raptor

Darius' Promise - Jen Talty
Simon's Promise - Leanne Tyler
Nash's Promise - Stacey Wilk
Spencer's Promise - Deanna L. Rowley
Logan's Promise - Kris Norris

Team Falco

Fighting for Esme - Jen Talty
Fighting for Charli - Leanne Tyler
Fighting for Tessa - Stacey Wilk
Fighting for Kora - Deanna L. Rowley
Fighting for Fiona - Kris Norris

Athena Project

Beck's Six - Desiree Holt

Victoria's Six - Delilah Devlin
Cygny's Six - Reina Torres
Fay's Six - Jen Talty
Melody's Six - Regan Black

Team Trojan
Defending Sophie - Desiree Holt
Defending Evangeline - Delilah Devlin
Defending Casey - Reina Torres
Defending Sparrow - Jen Talty
Defending Avery - Regan Black

Brotherhood Protectors Yellowstone World
Team Wolf
Guarding Harper - Desiree Holt
Guarding Hannah - Delilah Devlin
Guarding Eris - Reina Torres
Guarding Payton - Jen Talty
Guarding Leah - Regan Black

Brotherhood Protectors Yellowstone World
Team Eagle
Booker's Mission - Kris Norris
Hunter's Mission - Kendall Talbot
Gunn's Mission - Delilah Devlin
Xavier's Mission - Lori Matthews
Wyatt's Mission - Jen Talty

PROLOGUE

THIRTEEN MONTHS AGO...

"IF I'D KNOWN you were flying us in, Booker, I would have let that tango shoot me in the ass, the other night."

Captain Booker Hayes shook his head as the voice boomed behind him, the familiarity of it easing the restless twinge in his gut that had taken root the moment he'd been called in. The same sensation that had been saving his butt for the past fifteen years as part of the Flight Concepts Division, affectionately once called Seaspray. The guys who ferried Black Ops wherever they needed to go. Usually in the dead of night behind enemy lines, and often under fire, but... Booker tried to live by the old adage that if he wasn't living on the edge, he was just taking up space.

A motto, his buddy, Wyatt Bixby, also subscribed to. Though, the man took it to the next level as a seasoned Navy SEAL, and the one person who was bound to be Booker's pain in the ass this trip. Though, that was likely because he was also Booker's best friend.

Booker glanced over his shoulder, exaggerating his sigh as he thumbed at Gunnar Nielsen walking past. "Thinking Gunn's the real reason that didn't happen."

Wyatt placed his hand on his chest. "Ouch. That hurt, buddy."

"And here I thought you Spec Op guys only bled on the inside."

"Bullets sure. But words…" Wyatt coughed a few times to sell it. "They cut deep."

"Pretty sure there's a medic on board. I bet he's got some *Hello Kitty* Band-Aids in his kit."

"Could you get him? I'm bleeding out."

"Jackass." Booker gave Wyatt a shove. "What are you doing here? We were supposed to be going on vacation in…" He looked at his watch. "Two hours?"

"What the hell do you think I'm doing here? I got called in, the same as you."

"You've been planning this trip for months. It's bad enough I had to back out, but why didn't you just tell HQ to screw off when they handed out this last-minute mission?"

"Going rogue is your move, buddy. Not mine."

Booker scoffed. "When, exactly, have I gone rogue?"

Wyatt held up his hand. "Do you want them alphabetically or numerically? Because if it's numerically, I'll need my toes, too."

Booker resisted the smile tugging at his lips. Not that he purposely disobeyed orders, but being a pilot, he was able to get "creative" at times — fake bursts of static or claim the transmission wasn't received — when his superiors wanted him to bug out and leave his team behind. Not that he officially *had* a team, but he considered every soldier or agent he flew into a mission, his teammate. And he didn't leave anyone behind.

"Christ, bend the rules a few times…"

"Two dozen. And that's just the ones I know about." He punched Booker in his arm. "Knowing those were to save me and my team makes it harder to call you out, though."

"Not that hard. You just threatened to remove your boots so you could list them."

Wyatt sighed, looking around the carrier. "Guess neither of us is going to get lucky on that beach."

"Please, you weren't going to get lucky unless Kirby decided to show up."

"What the hell are you talking about? We're just casual. You know, friends with benefits."

"Right, and how many other girls have you been *casual* with since you started dating her?" He laughed

3

at Wyatt's glare. "Exactly. Not that it matters because your mouth does that little twitching thing whenever you say her name. Face it, Wyatt. You've got it bad for the girl."

"I really don't. Though, speaking of having it bad…" The bugger actually lifted his eyebrows a few times. "What happened the other night with your DEA lady, Agent Jensen? Because the way you two were tangled up on the dance floor…"

Special Agent Calliope Jensen or Callie to her friends. Talented. Fierce, and what would undoubtedly be a thorn in Booker's side for the rest of his life. The one who got away before he'd even had a chance to figure out if there was more than searing heat between them. If she might have been that once-in-a-lifetime kind of spark people always raved about.

Soul mates.

Which was crazy. Sure, Booker had known her for over a year, and had flown her and her various Joint Special Operation teams around more times than he cared to count. With both of them stationed in Virginia, they'd also met for coffee or gone out in groups whenever possible. And he wouldn't deny he'd worked hard to keep their relationship strictly professional — to look at her without wanting to sink his fingers into all that silky brown hair. Kiss those perfect full lips. See if she was just as feisty in bed as she was in the field. But he'd managed it — until the other night.

A few near-death experiences, and a couple too many tequilas, had resulted in some over-the-top slow dancing and the kind of kiss that shattered barriers. Demolished inhibitions. They'd managed to stumble back to her room — start getting serious — when she'd had to dart to the bathroom before slumping on the floor.

And he'd reined it all in. Carried her back to the bed then tucked her in before spending the night on the couch. Occasionally checking to ensure she hadn't suffered from alcohol poisoning or succumbed to some kind of allergic reaction he wasn't aware of. Getting called back to the base early — while she'd still been sleeping — hadn't done him any favors. He'd left her a note he'd hoped would have her calling him in record time, but...

It had been two days, and his phone hadn't so much as vibrated. Which was part of the reason his *spidey sense* was tingling because she'd grabbed him during one of his checks and told him how crazy she was about him. That she'd been waiting forever for him to finally make a move, and how she wanted so much more than just a quick tumble between the sheets.

He'd chalked it up to the liquor. To a life that probably mimicked his with too much work and too little time for any kind of relationship. Still, not having her call him after confessing she wanted so much more, stung.

5

Booker sighed. "Honestly, I don't know if we crashed and burned or if there's something else going on. Which implies drug dealers and secret missions. Either way, you can buy me a beer later, and I can cry into it."

Wyatt rolled his eyes. "She probably just got called into work. You don't always have to be so dramatic."

Booker grinned. "At least, I'm not still 'keeping it casual' with the lady I'm stupid in love with but don't have the balls to tell her."

"I already told you. I'm not in love with Kirby."

"Yeah, you are."

"Just, shut up, already. Jerk."

"Bitch."

"Who's a bitch?"

Booker turned, nodding at the man standing off to their left. Second Lieutenant John Calloway. FCD's newest recruit, and Booker's co-pilot. Though, if the rumors held any credence, the guy was cocky, arrogant, and had a severe hero complex. Not exactly the kind of pilot Booker enjoyed working with, but who was he to question the Air Force? Besides, this was a one-off for Booker. A favor when the regular pilot had contracted food poisoning and they'd been left scrambling. Why he suspected Wyatt's team had been called in, as well. Half of the SEALs had also gotten ill.

Booker ignored the prickling feeling still tingling along his spine as he shook Calloway's hand. "John.

Good to see you, again. This is Master Chief Wyatt Bixby. Wyatt, Second Lieutenant John Calloway. He's one of the new guys here at FCD."

John stared at Wyatt's hand for far too long, looking smug. "New isn't the term I'd use. I've been flying for over a decade, most of that with the Air Force." He gave Wyatt what appeared to be a reluctant handshake, all the while scowling as he scanned the ship. "Not quite what I thought it'd be. Hopefully, this isn't another taxi run. I was promised some action."

Wyatt glanced at Booker, arching his brow, and Booker could only shrug. He knew what his buddy was thinking. That the kid was already outing himself — playing the part of the lone wolf — the guy they should all be honored to have working with them. What would ostracize him if he didn't wise up — understand everyone was equal once bullets started flying. And they *always* started flying.

Booker cleared his throat. "Not sure how many taxi drivers get pelted with bullets, but then, I'm not from New York. And new just means you haven't worked in this division with these teams, before."

Calloway gave them both a scathing look. "Trust me, I've worked with these kinds of *teams* my entire career."

Wyatt took a calculated step forward, chest pushed out, hands fisted at his side. "What the hell's that supposed to mean?"

The man merely snorted. "Nothing... Master Chief."

Booker moved between them when his buddy took another step. "Easy, Wyatt." He turned to Calloway. "Just so we're clear. Bixby's been running Black Ops missions for longer than you've been in the service. He's commanded and survived more action than you'll ever get a chance to see, so... Show some respect."

When the guy just stood there, sneering, Booker leaned in. "Second Lieutenant."

Calloway muttered a hushed, "sir," then turned and headed inside— humming as if nothing had happened. That he hadn't just insulted one of the Navy's top SEAL team leaders.

Wyatt whistled, knocking Booker's shoulder. "Who the fuck picked that guy?"

"He's probably the hotshot son of someone important."

"He'd better wise up before Gunnar decides he needs a lesson in manners." He gave Booker another shove. "You didn't have to do that. Throw your weight around. I'm used to dealing with guys like him."

"No one disrespects one of *my* teammates. Period." Booker grinned at Wyatt. "And you are. My teammate. Maybe not all the time, but I take that seriously. Not that Calloway's attitude matters. Unless the jerk can somehow convince me in the next thirty minutes that he's worth me taking an interest in him — that this was all for show because he's the new kid — he's going to spend the entire flight watching me skim the treetops."

Wyatt laughed. "That's what I love about you, Booker. You're so nurturing."

"I'm a freaking den mother."

He motioned to the doorway, grinning when Wyatt blew him a few kisses before marching in. They gathered in the ready room, nodding at the rest of the men as everyone took a seat. Booker glanced at Calloway, shaking his head at how the guy had distanced himself. Not completely separate, but it was obvious he didn't consider himself part of the crew — a joint task encompassing eight SEAL members and six Rangers. All highly trained, looking like death dressed in black. The kind of men no one wanted gunning for them.

Which only made Calloway's behavior stand out. How he snubbed the gathering of men, heading for the helicopters as soon as the commander released them. Not even bothering to introduce himself or get a feel for the teams.

Gunnar sauntered over to Booker, scowling at Calloway's back as the guy left the ready room. "Who the fuck is the asshole wearing blues?"

Booker sighed. Gunnar wasn't one to pull punches and would definitely school Calloway if the guy didn't pull his head out of his ass. "New guy."

9

"He's going to be the *ex-guy* if he doesn't start playing nice in the sandbox."

Booker snagged Gunnar's arm. "I'll have a chat with him. Promise."

Gunnar snorted. "You're way too nice, Hayes. And the jerk's lucky he's got you as his partner. Just... don't be too sweet. I haven't gotten a reprimand for slugging an officer in some time."

"I'll keep your lack of a recent scarlet letter in mind." Booker headed out, eyeing Calloway as the guy walked around the machine, occasionally sneering at the men loading gear.

Wyatt moved in behind him, nudging his shoulder. "I'm sure he'll come around after he's gotten a couple of missions under his belt. For all we know, the cockiness is his way of covering his fear."

"Or he's a privileged asshole."

Wyatt laughed. "I think it's great the way you see the best in people."

"It's a gift." He headed for the machine, stopping when two men dodged in front of him, pretending they didn't see him until he'd damn near tripped over them as they cut him off.

Hunter "Wolf" Black and Xavier Larson. Hard core Army Rangers, though Booker knew Xavier had started out as a pilot before hanging up his wings for a sniper rifle. Not something Booker would ever willingly choose, but he respected the hell out of the other man for taking the chance.

Hunter threw himself onto the deck, rolling around for a few moments before allowing Xavier to help him up. Acting like a twelve-year old as he feigned a shoulder injury, shaking his head at Booker. "I think it's fatal."

"Doesn't that act ever get old, Hunter?"

The man took a stumbling step forward, still leaning on Xavier. "Nope. Just you, buddy."

"That so?" He inched closer. "I'm thinking the commander was wrong. I definitely feel a shit ton of turbulence rolling in."

Hunter grinned, reaching into his pocket before removing a feather. "Then, you're really gonna need this, Booker."

Booker laughed. Xavier and Hunter had been pulling the same, lame Dumbo joke for the past few years. Ever since they'd discovered Booker had been orphaned as a child and grown up in the system, hopping from one foster home to another before spending his last few years with a family who owned a carnival. Booker didn't think it was that funny, but the two knuckleheads seemed to get a kick out of it. And he knew it had morphed from a stupid prank into a ritual. What guaranteed a safe flight, including a trip home. And he'd be damned if he was the one to break the cycle. Not when it secretly made him feel better, too.

He took the feather, shaking his head. "I thought I had it inside me, all along?"

Hunter shrugged. "With the way you fly, I wouldn't chance it."

"Chance what?"

Booker groaned inwardly when Calloway moved in behind Xavier, hands on hips. Lips pursed. Still looking smug. "Just a friendly razzing. Xavier. Hunter. This is John Calloway. My co-pilot, today. John, meet two of the Rangers we're flying out."

Calloway gave them each a curt nod, not bothering to extend his hand. "Machine's ready." He crossed his arms over his chest. "Unless you don't trust me."

Great. Now Booker would look like a bastard if he insisted on doing his own checks. "It's never a matter of trust, Calloway. Just safety."

"So, that's a yes… To not trusting me."

Xavier looked between them, nudging Hunter.

The other man moved forward, offering Calloway another feather. "So Booker doesn't give you a hard time."

Calloway took the offering, staring at it as if he thought the men were crazy until they'd sauntered off before tossing it aside. "I'll be waiting in the chopper."

Booker closed his eyes, silently counting to ten, before glancing over at Wyatt. "I know. I'll deal with it before Gunnar slugs the guy."

Wyatt shrugged. "Oh, don't. Getting knocked to the ground might be what's needed. And Gunn's definitely the guy for the job. He really doesn't give a shit."

"I'll keep that in mind. You ready?"

"Please… This is a cakewalk compared to our last trip together."

"And now, you've jinxed it. Good thing I've got that feather."

"Jerk."

Wyatt gave Booker one final shove, angling toward the back as Booker did a quick walk around. Not that he didn't trust Calloway, but Booker had meant what he'd said. His teammates were counting on him safely delivering them to the landing zone, and crashing because one of them had missed an easy fix was a stupid way to die.

John gave him a scathing side eye as he jumped into his seat, running through part of the checklist before donning his helmet — clicking the mike. "I suppose you'll insist on flying."

Booker wouldn't yell. He had more control than that. "You got a problem with that?"

"I thought the whole reason for pairing me up with someone like you was to give me more experience."

"Or maybe, they're hoping you'll learn a few things. Like how to get along with your teams."

John scoffed. "I didn't say anything."

"That's the point. These men have enough to worry about without thinking their pilot's a jackass."

The muscle in Calloway's temple jumped. "Is that your official position, sir?"

"Consider it a friendly tip. How many times have you taken off from a carrier?"

The man snorted. "Plenty."

"Simulators don't count. I mean real world takeoffs."

That smug grin slipped a bit. "A dozen or so."

"So, like three." Booker ignored the man's glare. "I'll make you a deal. We're second in line. Show me you can anticipate Pierce's movements when he takes off in front of us — follow his lead — and I might let you fly us the whole way. But... If I change my mind for *any* reason, you don't hesitate to relinquish control. Are we clear?"

"Yes, sir."

"When it's just us, you don't have to call me sir. Just don't be a dick about it."

Booker shook his head as Calloway nodded, still glaring, before the man ran through the rest of the checks, readying the chopper for flight. Even as he started the machine, rolling on the throttle, Booker was second guessing himself. Aware the other man was right — he needed the experience — but not wanting to give up control. Not when that prickling along his neck hadn't eased. What felt like a full-on premonition that shit was about to go sideways.

The comms chirped, Captain Walker Pierce from the other helicopter calling in a warning light. What would either be a slight delay or a complete washout of the mission. Calloway glanced at Booker, but he merely shrugged, waiting as Pierce dealt with the situation.

Wyatt came over the comms. "Booker. Something wrong, buddy?"

Booker looked over his shoulder, keying up his mike. "Just waiting on a possible issue with Eagle One. We should know in a few minutes if the mission's a go."

Wyatt frowned but nodded, leaning forward to chat with the rest of his team. Normally, Booker would have been talking to the crew, laughing it up to keep them at ease, but with John scowling in the other seat, it hadn't felt right. And Booker didn't trust the other man not to relay anything he said to his superiors. Not that Booker really cared, but... He didn't need some greenhorn making waves. Causing issues because the guy was more interested in climbing the ladder than actually doing his job. Harsh, but Booker had witnessed it before. And John Calloway had it in spades.

Another five minutes, then Pierce was calling the tower — getting the green light. Booker slipped on his night vision goggles, nodding at Calloway as the man made one last check, giving Booker the thumbs up.

Booker looked out the window as Pierce eased his bird off the platform, adjusting for the gusting winds and the constant pitching of the deck. The guy had gained about fifteen feet, was dipping the helicopter forward to gain speed, when the machine rocked, swinging violently to the left before starting to spin.

"Shit. Calloway, get us airborne. Now."

Booker snapped his head toward the other man, cursing the man's parted lips and white knuckles, before grabbing the controls. "I have her."

He moved, yanking on the controls — countering the sudden increase in torque — as he lifted the chopper off the deck, dipping them back and sideways. Sliding left just as the other helicopter spun toward them, narrowly missing the tower before heading for the platform. Right where they'd been parked seconds earlier. What would have been a collision if he hadn't managed to move in time. Get them clear. There was a moment of silence. Of the machines dancing around each other, the surroundings blurring into that eerie shade of green, before the deck erupted into flames, burning everything a bright white.

Booker clawed the goggles off his face, fighting the controls as Calloway snapped out of his trance, nearly reefing the cyclic out of his hand. Sending them back through the billow of smoke.

"Damn it, John, let go!"

Calloway looked his way, goggles half off his face, eyes wide. Unseeing. Booker reached over just enough to knock him off the controls before doing his best to stabilize the machine — get them clear of the smoke before they plowed into the tower. Or worse...

Not that it helped. Two seconds in and the damn machine started shaking, tipping left and right as the inputs grew heavy. Stopped moving despite his efforts.

Hydraulics. What must have been the result of a perforated line.

Was the smoke thicker? Coming from inside? He couldn't tell. Didn't have time to worry when alarms blared through the cockpit, several of the gauges spiking into the red as the instrument panel lit up like a damn Christmas tree.

"Shit. Hold tight."

His voice barely registered above the noise. The shouts rising from the back. The chopper dipped, again, rocking sideways as the weight shifted, sending them sliding off to one side.

The men. That's what had changed. They were bouncing around in the back, darting left and right, making it impossible to find any kind of equilibrium. Not with the damn hydraulics gone. Nothing but sheer force left to move the controls.

Booker chanced a look behind him, instantly regretting it. Flames shot out one side of the chopper, bits of debris littered across the back. He wasn't sure when they'd gotten hit. If it had been when Calloway had been fighting him for control, or just now, when he'd swung back over because the machine wasn't responding. Regardless, he had no more than a few seconds to figure out his next move before other systems started failing.

He keyed up the mike, hoping the men could hear him above the chaos. "Grab onto something, gents, the ride's about to get bumpy—"

The chopper lurched then spun, sending them careening across the platform.

"And that's the tail rotor crapping out on us. No other choice but to put her in the water. When we hit, I'll try to tip her towards me, but... be ready for her to flip."

That's all he had time for before he was holding tight. Using every ounce of skill to keep her level as he let her spin until they were clear of the carrier — what would have taken out the row of jets lined up on the side and likely killed them all in the crash — before sending up a prayer then bottoming the collective. The machine stabilized for one precious moment — hanging in the air in that eerie slow-motion lag time that happened in the midst of a deadly crisis — before it dropped like a damn brick as it headed for the water.

Booker held firm, yanking up on the collective as they neared the surface. Doing his best to time everything perfectly. Until Calloway grabbed at the controls, again. Tipped them sideways just enough the waves caught one of the wheels — dragged them over.

Dead.

That's what they'd all be in exactly three seconds. As the blades hit the water, shooting off in different directions. Pieces of one crashing through the bubble — bits of the plexiglass spraying across the cockpit. Booker took a breath, grunting when he got slammed back into the seat, just as the machine flipped, the rush of water quickly pulling them down.

Every went black, the numbing cold stealing what little air he'd gulped in. He fumbled with his harness, finally unlatching the ends only to realize he was pinned, pieces of debris impaled through his shoulder and ribs then into the seat. He pulled at the ends, his fingers barely moving as dots ate up the edges of his vision.

His lungs burned, that small gasp of air nearly gone, when the door beside him rocked open, Wyatt grabbing him by the vest. He paused long enough yank the hunks of metal free before pulling Booker out then up. Water sprayed across his face as they crested the waves, sucking in a lungful of air.

Wyatt wrapped one arm around his shoulders, keeping them both from sinking back down. "Breathe, buddy."

Booker wanted to tell him he was trying. That he'd spent his entire life breathing, only the words wouldn't form right. Not when it felt as if some bastard was cracking his chest open with every failed breath.

Wyatt cursed. "Fuck, you're really bleeding. Talk to me, Booker. Can you breathe?"

He glanced over his shoulder, managing a rough, "Barely," before closing his eyes. Doing his best to keep kicking. Keep floating. Not that Wyatt was fairing much better. Booker had gotten a glimpse of his buddy's leg — how his knee wasn't pointing in the right direction. Not to mention the blood on the back of the man's hand or the obvious lump on his head.

Wyatt coughed, dipping under for a second before pushing back up. "Boats are on their way. Just… stay with me."

Booker nodded, finally taking stock of the men bobbing in the water around him. Knowing there weren't enough heads to account for every teammate. In fact, other than Gunnar, Xavier, and Hunter, he wasn't sure who had made it out, not that the men were unscathed. Even half-conscious, Booker saw the burns on Gunnar. What looked like more on Hunter, though, with only their heads and shoulders out of the water, it was hard to tell if the blood and wounds were from the fire or the crash. But there was no mistaking how all the men were bleeding. Barely keeping themselves above the crushing waves. "Calloway…"

Christ, it hurt to talk. To get just that one word out.

Wyatt sighed, coughing up more water. "I couldn't... One of the blades... He was already gone."

The words hit Booker hard, and he had to fight not to sink back down. Join the wreckage because... it was his fault. It didn't matter that he'd done his best — avoided getting crushed beneath the other chopper. Fought to keep it upright — to keep it together. All he knew was that he'd failed. Had broken his promise to always bring his teammates back alive.

That, when they'd really needed him, he hadn't been enough.

Wyatt squeezed his arm. "Don't. Don't start second guessing everything. You kept us in the game. That's all we can ask."

"I should..."

He should have done more. Knocked Calloway out or found a way to land on the damn carrier.

"Just... shut up and breathe. Because if you even think about dying on me..."

Booker nodded, aware he wouldn't be that lucky. Wouldn't get a quick and easy reprieve. That, for better or worse, he'd spend the next fifty years atoning for a sin he'd never be able to undo.

CHAPTER 1

Present Day, West Yellowstone, Montana, BHP Aviation Division...

Booker banked the chopper to the left, skimming it over the trees, grinning at how the downwash fluttered the leaves. What looked to be another stunning day, with blue skies and warm temperatures.

One of the many reasons to enjoy the view before everything turned cold and white. What would be his first full winter in Montana.

His headset chirped a moment before Wyatt's voice echoed through the comms. "You do know this is only an exercise, right?"

Booker chuckled. "What's the matter, buddy? You going soft on me?"

"Maybe I'd just like to make it to the *infil* point without you plowing us into the trees."

"I'm not going to plow us into the trees. Though, you have a point. I should make this more realistic, since Hank didn't want to have people *actually* firing at us today."

"Booker, I didn't… shit."

Booker's other occupant cursed as Booker banked in the opposite direction, rushing them past the edge of a cliff before pulling back on the cyclic — climbing over an old fire tower only to drop them down the other side as he followed the curve of the rock face.

Booker keyed up his mike. "Stone? You okay back there?"

Stone Jacobs. Head of the Brotherhood Protector's Yellowstone division and one of Booker's bosses. The other, Hank Patterson, was still back at their new base, undoubtedly watching the exercise unfold. Though, based on the white in Stone's knuckles, Booker bet his ass Stone wished he'd stayed behind, too.

Stone shook his head. "You definitely live up to your reputation, Hayes. Though, I'm with Bixby. You don't have to kill us in order to prove you've still got a great set of hands."

"Please, this is just for the sheer fun of it. *Infil* point coming up in twenty seconds. You gents best get ready."

He leveled off, heading for the clearing in front of

them, ignoring the way Stone's words echoed in his head. After months of rehab, and more than a few therapy sessions, Booker was doing his best to let go of the past. To find forgiveness when the guilt still hovered out of sight. Waiting for a chance to rear its ugly head. Remind him of all the ways he'd failed that fateful night before being medically discharged a few months later.

That, despite his new job — his new life — nothing had changed. That he was still the reason good men had died.

A flash of smoke and flames — of churning water and utter darkness — wavered in the distance, but he blinked it away. He could question his worth later... after he'd completed the training exercise. Done exactly what Stone had claimed and proven to himself he was good enough.

A glance out the bubble, a shift of the controls, and Booker brought the machine into a high hover. "Area's clear. You gents are good to go."

Wyatt keyed up his mike. "See you back at base, buddy."

He grinned, holding everything steady as Wyatt and Stone repelled to the ground then raced to a waiting vehicle, giving Booker the thumbs up before he peeled away, allowing Xavier to have his turn at the clearing.

Booker had to hand it to the other man. He'd taken back to flying full time without hesitation. And the guy was good. Better than good, actually. What could have been a career in the FCD if he'd wanted, though Booker suspected a part of the guy still missed his Ranger days. But, like the rest of the men who had survived the double crash, that part of their lives had come to a screeching halt.

Thankfully, Hank had tossed them all a lifeline when one of his employees had heard Booker talking about starting his own airline. Though, Hank had taken it to a whole other level. Booker had been thinking two or three choppers. Maybe a crappy little office on the side. A few of buddies to round out a crew. Hank had manufactured an impressive facility with enough machines to keep him, Xavier, and a couple more pilots busy until they were ready to retire.

But it wasn't just Booker and Xavier who Hank had saved. Wyatt, Gunnar, Hunter... Walker Pierce and the survivors from the other chopper. Hank had offered them all positions in his new division, which was quickly shaping up to see almost as much action as Booker had seen in the military. Just yesterday, he'd flown shotgun with Wyatt and Hunter on a protection detail, and they'd been fired at more than once.

Exactly what he'd needed to ease any lingering doubts. That, with a bit of time and a whole lot of luck, he might just make it fully to the other side of the accident still intact. Still sane.

Mostly sane, if he didn't count his unhealthy obsession over a particular DEA agent. The one who *still* hadn't called him back. Who he couldn't get out of his mind and secretly feared might be in trouble but had absolutely no way of unearthing if or where that trouble would be. If he should be riding to the rescue or taking the giant ass hint that she hadn't meant what she'd said that night. That the constant itching between his shoulder blades had nothing to do with her life being in jeopardy and everything to do with his life going sideways.

Not that he'd mention any of his concerns to his crew or his bosses, especially Hank Patterson. Ex-Navy SEAL, and the guy standing beside the helipad as Booker made his approach — coming in hot before flaring back, mindful to keep the downwash to a minimum as he landed the chopper, then shut her down, grinning when he finally climbed out. He had to hand it to Hank, the man had great instincts. Had chosen the kind of equipment Booker would have picked if asked.

Hank shook his head as Booker made his way over, watching the vehicles head toward them in the distance. "And here I thought civilian life would take some of that dangerous streak out of you."

Booker chuckled. "Sorry, but that's just part of my DNA. Besides, if yesterday is any indication of how the next decade is going to pan out, I'll need all of that craziness and then some."

"Ain't that the truth. Which means Pierce and the others will test my sanity just as much once they're ready to come on board. Though, I'm hoping Xavier has a bit more self-preservation."

Booker nudged Hank's arm when Xavier raced toward them, fifty feet off the deck with twin dust eddies whirling behind him as he waited until the last moment to bleed off all the airspeed and plunk the machine down across the large red H. "Right. He's far calmer than me."

"I should have known you'd all be the reason for more gray hairs."

"Thinking that's how you like it." He nodded at the man. "I can't thank you enough for this. Seriously… Not sure what we would have done if you hadn't tossed us this Hail Mary."

Hank waved it off as if it was nothing. That it was perfectly normal to create massive infrastructure on what felt like a whim to Booker. "I'd been considering it for a while. I just didn't have the personnel to make it a reality until you brought it up during the last of your rehab at Brighter Days Ranch. I'm just glad Taz ratted you guys out, or I might have missed a huge opportunity."

"Thinking we're the ones who would have missed out, but thanks, just the same."

A snort. As if Hank thought Booker was crazy, which, he probably was. Not that Booker would point that out. Give Hank a reason to reconsider keeping Booker as part of the team. But the fact Hank seemed unfazed by everything that had happened eased any remaining tension.

Two SUVs pulled up as the rest of the men disembarked.

Hank raised a brow when Stone moved in beside him. "Well? How'd they do?"

"Picture perfect, as expected. Though, remind me to fly with Xavier, next time. I like keeping my lunch in my gut and not up in the back of my throat."

Booker placed a hand on his chest. "Are you seriously saying you didn't enjoy those maneuvers? That hurts, Stone."

"Not nearly as much as my stomach when you dropped us off that cliff — gave me a real closeup view of all those rocks. You definitely have some mad skills, Booker. Still…"

Xavier clapped Booker on the shoulder as he ran over from his machine. "I don't know where you learned some of those moves, but damn… you're a hard man to keep up with."

"Says the guy who flies as if he was born in a cockpit. But, it's nice to know someone appreciates my flying style."

Gunnar nudged Wyatt. "Yeah, the jackass who never has to fly with him."

Booker shook his head. "You, too, Gunn?"

Gunn merely shrugged. "Like Stone said. You've

got some mad skills, but you definitely like to take things to the extreme."

"Just give Xavier a couple more months, and he'll be as crazy as me. Guaranteed."

Hunter huffed. "Do *not* encourage the guy. I only have so many feathers."

Booker patted his breast pocket. "Still got mine, so… feel free to give Xavier the lion's share."

"And miss throwing myself on the ground in front of you? I don't think so."

Gunn sighed. "You're all nuts. Though, those crazy skills of yours, Booker, are the only reason any of us are alive to tease you. What you did that night…"

Booker rolled his shoulders. He hated when the guys thanked him for what had happened. Not when he knew if he'd been half the pilot he thought he was, he would have found a way to ensure everyone had survived. It was bad enough they had all suffered injuries — Burns. Dislocations. Permanent numbness, not to mention lingering migraines and vertigo. But knowing they'd been medically discharged because of them stung more. Just like his discharge for a pneumothorax and a left side that didn't quite work right.

He waved it off. "You four are the reason we got out of that chopper alive. Getting those doors open, then getting everyone you could out, despite being upside down and twenty feet below the water. Not to mention Wyatt pulling that metal out of my side and shoulder then dragging my ass to the surface. All I did was keep the machine in one piece long enough to ditch it."

Gunn sighed. "A lesser man wouldn't have even gotten us airborne. Would have froze like Calloway did. You had what? Three seconds to get us clear? And that doesn't include how you had to fight Calloway for most of that time. When we started spinning... I still don't know how you kept it level and upright. How you avoided hitting any of those jets. I'm just glad Hank opted to start this division because I really didn't want to see what your idea of an airline looked like."

Xavier laughed. "Knowing Booker, it would have been a makeshift C-Can and a couple of choppers that were always being *tinkered* with."

Booker crossed his arms on his chest, ignoring the pinch in his ribs that never quite vanished. How the scar tissue always pulled when he moved. "I'd be thoroughly insulted if that wasn't exactly what I had in mind. Though, if you all prefer a state-of-the-art facility with shiny new machines..."

"Speaking of which..." Hank motioned to the building standing like a monolith against the mountainous backdrop. "Let's head in. Now that you've all had a few days to get acquainted with the machinery and the kinds of jobs you'll be facing, it might be a good time to go over any questions. Make sure we have everyone's documents on file, in case we get an emergency call. With Booker's contact overseas squared away, I've been able to open this division to international endeavors. I have a feeling you guys are going to be very busy."

The men started for the main doors, joking and shoving each other. Booker lagged behind, doing his best to overlook the way they didn't quite move as fluidly as they once had. The occasional limp or how Xavier shook his hand a few times to ease what Booker knew was residual numbness. Just like he knew Hunter self-medicated with exercise and beer to deal with his chronic pain.

What they'd all come to accept as the cost of surviving. The basis for moving forward.

And if that meant Booker bought the first round of beers to quiet his demons that night, he embraced it. An acceptable means of shoving all those lingering memories down until he'd need a spotlight to go hunting for them. Letting the alcohol soothe the restless feeling on the back of his neck that was more than his unresolved concerns over Calliope. This was the kind of nagging that had always warned him when shit was about to go sideways. Like that night, when he hadn't been able to shake the itchy sensation between his shoulder blades.

He leaned against the bar, scanning the room, but if someone was watching him, they were doing a damn fine job of staying hidden. Which only made that irritating voice inside his head scream a bit louder. That edginess scratch at his conscience a bit harder.

"Booker. Buddy, are you okay?"

He stopped scouring the crowd long enough to glance at Wyatt — give the man a nod. "Aces. Why?"

Wyatt scoffed, grabbing one of the beers the bartender placed in front of Booker. "You've got that look."

"The one that says I'm about to kick your ass at darts? Hell, yeah."

Wyatt gave him a slight side eye. "The one that says you're about to crawl out of your skin."

Trust his friend to see through the bullshit. "Thinking maybe it's time to cut you off."

"You know I don't drink that much, and never enough to read you wrong. We've been friends too long, and before you lie to my face — again — you've had it since we walked in here. Something you need to tell me?"

"Like what?"

"I don't know. Maybe those voices are talking a bit too loud inside your head. Ever since Gunn mentioned the accident, you've been distant. I know that's one of your triggers — having anyone thank you for keeping us alive that night, but I think it's more than that. This… this is like that spooky woo woo crap we've all had once or twice. So, I'll ask you, again. There something you need to tell me?"

"Not if you think I've got woo woo crap inside my head."

"That's not what I meant, and you know it. Stop deflecting."

"It's nothing, I just…" He glanced around the room, again, as he rolled his shoulders. "Ever get the feeling you're being watched?"

"Yeah. For the entire time I was a SEAL." Wyatt leaned in closer. "You sensing something?"

"It's probably nothing, but ever since we left the facility, I can't shake the prickling on the back of my neck."

Wyatt nodded, taking another swig before casually scanning the bar without *looking* as if he was scanning it. "Nothing jumps out at me, but… We'll keep an eye out. If your instincts are telling you someone's following you…"

"Probably just residual paranoia from getting shot at yesterday. It's been a hot minute since I've been involved in active fire."

"You and me both, brother. Still, I'd rather we make fools of ourselves, than get caught with our pants down."

"What's the matter, buddy? Feeling a bit… inadequate?"

"I'm not the one going home to an empty bed."

"And you aren't? Unless… Don't tell me. Kirby's dropping by for a visit."

"If she actually dragged herself away from her

gorillas long enough to jump on the damn plane, she should be landing in a couple of hours."

"Then, why are you still drinking? You don't want to have any... issues."

"This is only my second. Pretty sure I won't have any *issues*. Though, it's sweet you're worried about me."

"More that Kirby might kick your ass if you're down and out."

"You really are a jackass, you know that?"

"At least, I'm not still pretending I'm not in love."

Wyatt sighed, though, Booker didn't miss the way the corner of his mouth quirked, or the slight slash of red across his cheeks.

"Shit. You *really* are in love with her, aren't you? Seriously, in love." Booker shook his head at Wyatt's glare. "I was mostly teasing all those other times. I mean, you have a tell, but christ... You're not even trying to hide it."

"Shut up."

Booker glanced around the bar, still nursing that prickling feeling along his neck. "You need to tell her. You know that, right?"

"It's complicated."

"It really isn't."

Wyatt huffed. "How about we focus on your pathetic love life, instead?"

"Can't focus on nothing."

"You need to date. Or, at least, invite a lady home

with you." He shook his head when Booker merely stared at him. "When's the last time you kissed someone?"

Booker chuckled, moved in as he palmed Wyatt's jaw then planted a big sloppy kiss on the man's face. "There. Happy?"

Wyatt wiped the corner of his mouth, shaking his head. "I seriously hope that's not how you kiss the ladies because I'd understand why you're alone."

"I've seen you kiss, and that was a thousand times better than what your sorry mouth can do."

"You're not wrong, Booker, but he does have a certain charm."

Booker startled, hating the fact he automatically reached for his gun before he had the good sense to stuff his hand in his pocket — pray it didn't look half as silly as it had felt. Kirby Carrington stood several feet away, one foot tapping the old wood floors as she alternated her gaze between them. Her long blonde hair pulled back in some kind of messy bun, her blue-green eyes focused on Wyatt. And Booker couldn't help but wonder if she even noticed anyone else in the room.

Sure, Wyatt had claimed she was the one who was keeping their relationship at arm's length, but looking at her now... She certainly didn't appear unaffected by his buddy's presence.

He nodded toward Wyatt. "I'm not sure charm is in Wyatt's vocabulary."

Wyatt gave him a swat, moving over to her before dropping a quick kiss on her lips. "I thought I was picking you up?"

Kirby laughed, tucking a few loose strands of hair behind her ear. "I was able to get on an earlier connection. Figured it was just easier to catch a cab. Though, if I'd known I'd walk in on the love fest between you two..."

Wyatt waved it off. "Booker was just being an ass."

Booker scoffed. "You don't have to be mean because we both know I'm the better kisser."

"In your dreams, buddy."

Kirby sighed. "Now I know why I always suspected there were three of us in our bed." She pointed to the beers. "One of those for me?"

Wyatt grinned, and fuck, Booker swore the guy was beaming. Actually beaming. As if she'd started a fire inside of him and it was seeping out through his skin. And there was no missing the dopey-eyed way he stared at Kirby. The guy had it bad. "Definitely."

Wyatt handed her a bottle, glancing over at Booker but he simply grinned, ordering another before joining them at the table. There was casual conversation and some good-natured teasing with the crew before the others went off to shoot darts, leaving him, Wyatt and Kirby at the table.

Booker nodded at Kirby. "So, Kirby. I have to say, I don't think any lady's traveled a few thousand miles to visit me."

Kirby laughed. "It's not just to see Wyatt. My parents are celebrating their fortieth wedding anniversary. They live close by, so I'm doing double duty."

"They live outside West Yellowstone?"

"Salt Lake City, actually."

He managed to school his features before he let his mouth hinge open because his idea of close wasn't three hundred miles and over four hours of driving. But who was he to judge? "Quite the accomplishment for them. How's work? Your gorillas okay?"

She shrugged, downing the last of her beer. "Better, now that we've dealt with this stupid poaching ring. Bastards were stealing the babies for meat. Sick, really."

Had he choked on his beer? Spit it across the table? Or was Wyatt the only one slamming a fist on his chest to keep from coughing. "You did what, now?"

She shrugged off his question. "It was nothing. We just took turns photographing the assholes before turning it over to the police. They staged a raid and now, things are better."

Booker had to give Wyatt credit. The guy didn't yell. Didn't react at all for a good thirty seconds before calmly tapping her shoulder —gaining her attention.

Wyatt cleared his throat, his other hand fisted so tightly around his beer bottle, Booker was surprised the damn thing didn't shatter. "You took photographs? Of the poachers?"

Kirby sighed. "We deal with poachers all the time. This ring was just a bit nastier than usual. Maybe a bit more organized, but..." She held up her hand to stop him from interrupting. "The police did all the work. We merely provided them with the evidence to get the job done."

"And did they? Get the job done?"

"I just said it was better."

"Better doesn't mean the threat's been eliminated. Did they arrest everyone?"

"I think so. I don't know, I wasn't there when they raided their camp. All I know is that it's been a few weeks, and it's been quiet. So, yeah, I think they got everyone."

"Or maybe some of the bastards are hiding, biding their time until they think it's safe to retaliate."

"Why would anyone retaliate when they can simply move to another location where they won't catch any grief? We're fine."

Wyatt looked over at him, and Booker knew exactly what his buddy was thinking. That things weren't over until he and Wyatt had gone through everything and ensured the local cops hadn't missed anyone.

Booker nudged Kirby. "I don't suppose you have a copy of that evidence?"

Her frown deepened. "We gave it all to the cops. Why?"

"We just like to be thorough. Occupational hazard."

"It's been taken care of. Period. Can we talk about something else? Like where your date's hiding?"

Wyatt chuckled, though Booker heard the slight edge to it. How his buddy wasn't close to wanting to discuss something else. "Yeah, buddy. Where's your date?"

Booker sighed, forcing a smile. "It's like you two share a brain. I don't have one, unless Wyatt wants to let me slap another kiss on him." He leaned toward Kirby, motioning to Wyatt with a nod. "I can arm wrestle you for him."

She laughed. "Now I know why Wyatt thinks you're an ass."

"I am an ass. But I'm an adorable one."

"You're something." She slid her finger along the bottle, looking as if she wasn't sure if she wanted to say something before meeting his gaze. "So, whatever happened to Calliope? You two looked pretty cozy the last time I saw you."

"I guess she just wasn't that into me."

"Seriously? You think she wasn't that into you? Are all men this dense?"

"It's been a year, Kirby. Even I can take that kind of message."

"Don't get me wrong, Booker, I'd usually agree

but… The girl was more than a bit into you. She had it bad. Maybe she's just been busy at work? It can't be easy being in the DEA, doing regular stints into Mexico. And with you sidelined for a while, then moving out here…"

"I guess that's possible."

"But you don't think so. Have you tried calling her?"

"A few times, but it's always the same answer. She's unavailable. No idea when she'll *be* available."

Wyatt thumbed the lip of his beer. "You think she's in trouble?"

"I think she knows how to find me if she wants to, so… Another round?"

He got up, ignoring the clench in the pit of his stomach. That scratchy feeling on his neck that wouldn't go away. Not when Wyatt's words echoed in his head. How Booker had been harboring concerns for longer than he cared to admit.

Not that it mattered. He'd been serious. He'd tried her office more than a few times, but no one was talking. And the inquiries he'd made on the side — the favors he'd called in — hadn't gotten him any answers. Which only made him feel like a stalker.

He grabbed some more beers, then managed to make idle conversation for another thirty minutes before they all headed home, that uneasy feeling shadowing his every move. The fact his front entrance was shrouded in darkness suddenly dawned on him that he'd left himself wide open for an attack. That he should have insisted on the manager installing perimeter lighting. That somewhere between going to rehab and his new job, Booker had let some of his training slide.

A mistake he'd correct in the morning. Along with a full spectrum of security cameras and motion sensors. How he should have outfitted the apartment the moment he'd signed the rental agreement. Of course, being in the middle of nowhere Montana had dulled his natural paranoia. What seemed like the most unlikely place for anything sinister to crop up.

Christ, maybe he was the one who'd gone soft.

He took a deep breath, giving the area the once-over before he jumped out of his truck and made for the door, his head on a swivel. Muscles primed because that prickling sensation had grown into a full-on premonition — just like the night of the accident. Was practically slapping him upside the head, and he'd be damned if he ignored another warning.

He made it all the way to his front door — had the key in the lock — when the air stirred behind him. A duck and a spin, and he had the person by the arm — was shifting off the his right. Another step and a shove and the hooded figure was pinned to the door. Hood falling back. Her ruby-red lips lifted into a bemused grin.

He froze, staring into those killer blue eyes as his heart skipped a beat. "Calliope?"

She levered up, breaking his hold before pivoting to the left — using her feet to trip him onto his ass. He hit hard, stones biting into his back a second before she was on top of him. Hips locked around his torso. Her weight shifted forward just enough he couldn't buck her off.

She locked her fingers around his wrists, leaning in close — all that silky brown hair falling in a curtain around him — before that wicked mouth of hers lifted. "Hello, Booker. We need to talk."

CHAPTER 2

AFTER ALL THESE MONTHS, it was actually him. Booker Hayes. In the flesh. And he looked better than ever.

Special Agent Calliope Jensen bit her bottom lip, using the slight hurt to focus on the job at hand. How she needed to persuade Booker to be her unofficial partner — follow her into what would undoubtedly be hostile territory with only each other and whatever he could acquisition as backup.

Not that she was worried he'd say no. If there was one thing she'd learned about Booker after over a year of working with him, it's that he was the proverbial white knight. Only he rode in a helicopter instead of on a horse. The kind of man who'd jump first, worry if it got him killed, later. At least, she hoped he was still that guy.

She'd heard about the accident. Months later,

and at a time when she couldn't so much as send him a text. But she'd ached inside. Had nearly broken her cover a dozen times wanting nothing more than to call him. See if he was okay. If he needed her.

Which seemed stupid, seeing how things had turned out. She knew about the Brotherhood Protectors. Had colleagues who'd worked with some of the men the organization hired. All ex-military. Ex-special forces. So, for Booker to be heading their new aviation department meant he'd landed on his feet. Had clawed his way back and made a home for himself.

That, maybe, she was the only one who'd been agonizing over having to leave. Not being able to contact him.

That he hadn't wanted more.

Booker tensed beneath her before he smiled, easing back on the small walkway as if it was natural to be lying across the concrete. As if women jumped him every night of the week. And, maybe they did because... Damn, he was even hotter than she remembered. Chestnut-colored hair that sat in a tousled mess since dumping him on his ass. Enough scruff shadowing his jaw it was basically a beard, and a mouth she knew could take her from zero to a hundred in six seconds flat.

But those eyes... not quite blue, but not quite green. She'd never seen that particular shade before and just staring into them, now… it more than took her breath away.

"Ya know, I've had women take a while to call me back before. Some bullshit about dating rules. But at thirteen months, you definitely hold the record."

And just like that, any reservations vanished because he was definitely the guy she remembered. Sure, there was a haunted shadow in his eyes — what she suspected were demons or ghosts from that night when he'd almost died — but beneath that, he was pure action hero.

She leaned in, stopping with her mouth a breath away from his. "I've been a bit busy."

"Right." He moved, somehow sliding to the right, getting one arm beneath her ass, then flipping them. Using his other hand to cushion her head before he was lying on top of her, every inch of their bodies touching.

He mimicked her position, his breath mixing with hers. "Does that mean you're not busy, now?"

She relaxed against the pavement, giving him a genuine smile. "It's complicated."

"In other words, nothing's changed."

He eased back, rolling off then gaining his feet and offering his hand. Pulling her firmly against him before scanning the area. "You're the one who's been following me, right?"

She nodded, not surprised he'd picked up on her surveillance. She'd made sure he hadn't actually spotted her, but she'd guessed by the way he'd kept checking his six, that he'd sensed someone was shadowing him. "Unless you've pissed off some lover's husband."

"That would imply I've had other lovers."

Was that relief warming her skin? Or just being this close to the man she suspected she'd been halfway in love with before her entire world had imploded. Because hearing him suggest he hadn't been making the rounds of all the available women since she'd finally gotten a taste of him that one night did weird things to her head. Had her thinking of a life beyond the DEA. One where she surrounded herself with people she trusted.

Booker took another look around then motioned to the door. "We should take this inside, just to be safe. Key's in the lock."

She turned, then paused. Not because she didn't trust Booker, but because she'd spent nearly a year having to cover her own six. Never venturing into a room first. Always making sure no one could jump her from behind. That she always had an out. And just thinking about heading inside with him lagging behind had her breath stalling in her chest. The hairs on the back of her neck standing on end.

Booker sighed, his breath caressing her cheek as he leaned in close. "How long were you under?"

She pushed at the memories flickering in her head. The smell of accelerant. The echoed pops of gunfire mixing with the thunder. The disjointed voices as she'd slipped into unconsciousness. She knew it wasn't real. That, for the moment, she was safe.

She swallowed. Hard. "Eleven months."

Another sigh as he gave her arms a light squeeze. "Shit. I'll go in. Follow when you can."

He moved out from behind her, giving her a wide smile before unlocking his door then heading inside. Leaving it open. No other questions. No odd looks, just that smile, then him disappearing. As if her having a mini panic attack at the thought of him walking through a door behind her was normal. Something that happened to everyone, just like her waylaying him on the walkway — tripping him onto his back.

That he didn't see her as a freak.

Callie took a deep breath, then headed for the doorway, pausing long enough to gather her composure before stepping into his apartment. It was neat. Clean, but void of any personal items. As if he'd unpacked just enough to get by without fully committing. And she couldn't help but wonder if he was searching for something that felt like home, too? Something more than endless nights lying awake, praying to make it to the next day still intact. Still sane.

Glasses clinked in the distance, then he was strolling into the room, placing one on the counter as he slid onto the bar stool off to the right, leaving the left for her. She closed the door, glancing at the dead-bolt — unsure if she should lock it or not — before shaking her head then picking her way across the room. She checked her six one more time — still undecided if she should have locked the damn door — then eased onto the stool.

She arched a brow and took a cautious sip of the drink. "You just happened to have white rum, lime juice, and mint leaves in your fridge?"

"And you wouldn't?"

"Of course, I would. I love Mojitos, but I thought you were more of a whiskey guy."

He simply shrugged. "Not tonight."

Christ, had he kept the mixers for her favorite cocktail handy? In case she ever dropped by? Was she crazy to even consider that as an option? She stared at him, wondering if he'd relived their one night together as many times as she had, or if he'd merely brushed it off. Moved on after a few days had passed and she hadn't called him back.

She'd wanted to. More times than she could count, but it hadn't been possible, and she'd been left living in limbo. Unable to move forward but unwilling to forget.

Booker sighed, gently nudging her arm. "You're not the only one haunted by ghosts, so try to relax. Breathe. And, when you're ready, you can tell me the reason behind the surprise visit, because as much as my ego wants to think you're still as crazy about me as I am about you, I have a feeling it's something deeper. Darker."

He was crazy about her? *Is* crazy about her? Had he really just said that, or had she drifted off? Imagined the entire conversation because she was so damn tired of pushing through life. Pretending she was okay when she hadn't been able to move past the raid. That horrible night when everything had changed.

When she'd changed.

And not for the better.

"Callie? Sweetheart, you really need to take a few deep breaths before you pass out."

She blinked, realizing she'd been staring at him without speaking, with what she could only imagine was some spooky expression on her face. The kind that confirmed whatever thoughts were whirling inside his head. Those ghosts he'd mentioned.

It was too much. The way he furrowed his brow, looking as if he was ready to slay whatever demons she threw at him. She'd been right. He'd ride to the rescue, just like he always had. And she'd be the reason he got killed. She was *always* the reason people got killed.

She pushed to her feet, nearly tripping as she took a hurried step back. "Shit. I shouldn't have come. I can't ask... It's too risky..."

She turned, making a beeline for the door when

he hooked her elbow, spinning her against the wall. He moved in close, pinning her without actually touching her, one hand by her head, the other beside her waist. He didn't speak, just leaned in, his mouth dangerously close, again.

She could kiss him. All it would take was a small shift forward, and her lips would be touching his. His soft skin pressed against her mouth. A slide of her tongue across his flesh, and she knew he'd take control. Deepen the kiss until everything else vanished.

Booker cocked his head to the side as if he was following her train of thought. Knew how badly she wanted him to hold her. Tell her everything was going to be okay, even if it was a lie.

Instead, he inched closer, his body now skimming hers. "I let you go once when neither of us had any options. I pride myself on not making the same mistakes twice. So, take a breath, then tell me what the hell has you so spooked, because sweetheart, I know when someone's running scared, and you've got it in spades."

She huffed, hating that he saw through her so easily. That the walls she erected for everyone else crumbled around him with nothing more than his smile. "Believe me. Allowing me to walk out of here would *not* be a mistake."

"Like I said — you're not walking, you're running.

And it'd be a colossal mistake if you're in half as much trouble as I think you are."

And there it was. His armor shining in the overhead lights. All that honor radiating off him in waves. She relaxed against the wall, wondering if he would change his mind once he knew the extent of what she was asking.

She wet her lips, nearly giving-in to the need to kiss him when his gaze slipped to her mouth before sliding back up. "In a nutshell? I need a partner. Someone I can trust. Who I'm confident can't be bought. Who won't balk at flying a chopper in questionable conditions in a foreign country. Who can back me up on the ground when things inevitably go sideways. Who has a contact who can acquire a few *key* items. And who isn't afraid to break some rules if it means bagging the bad guys."

She leaned toward him, brushing her lips across his. "So, Booker... Do you know anyone like that?"

He stared at her, mouths barely touching before he grinned. "A name springs to mind, assuming he's free. Does this guy get to know where to have your *key* items delivered, which I'll surmise is code for a helicopter, vehicles, and a variety of weapons?"

She swallowed, ignoring the instant echo of gunfire in her mind. The damn voices that never stopped screaming inside her head. "That would be the minimum I'd want, seeing as it's San Juan."

"Puerto Rico? I thought you only went under-cover in Mexico? Where you knew all the players."

She simply shrugged. "I got reassigned."

"I see. Isn't it the rainy season in Puerto Rico, right now?"

"Wettest month of the year with the real possibility of hurricanes."

"Sounds lovely. And by bad guys, I assume you mean drug dealers with guns."

She snorted. "Are there any other kind?"

"Not generally. And I'll also assume that backing you up on the ground is because you can't fly directly to wherever it is you're going. Due to these bad guys with guns."

"Of course, I can't fly directly to their shack. That would be suicidal."

"Thought as much. Which means, at some point, you and this *partner* will be running through the jungle being chased by these bad guys... With guns."

She grinned. "Why else would anyone run through the jungle?"

"No other reason, really." He eased back slightly. "Yeah. I know a guy who meets those qualifications."

"Don't forget the most important part."

He arched a brow.

She swallowed, again, nearly choking on it. "The one where he can't be bought. Is someone I can trust with my life."

That brow furrowed, his gaze sweeping over her. "He'd be a pretty shitty guy if that wasn't the number one reason to rely on him. So, yeah, Calliope. You can trust him with your life. Be assured that, if anyone wants to get to you, they'll have to go through him, because he always brings his teammates home alive..."

He cleared his throat, those shadows in his eyes staring back at her. "Well, you get the gist. Just answer me one last question..."

"What's that?"

"How much time do I have to pack?"

She pursed her lips to hold back the giddy laugh threatening to claw free. The overwhelming sense of relief that, maybe, she'd finally unearth the bastard who'd set up her team — left her for dead. That, with a whole lot of luck, she might just make it back alive.

Callie stuffed her hand in her jacket pocket, removing two tickets to San Juan. The ones she'd bought before she'd had time to consider that he might turn her down. That she'd have to go alone. She held them up. "Not long if we're going to make our flight."

He took the tickets, looking at her when he realized his name was on one of them, before nodding. He stepped back, motioning to the stool. "Guess that's my cue to start packing while you finish your drink."

Booker gave her one last once-over then headed

for the hallway. He stopped when she called his name, glancing at her over his shoulder.

She tilted her head, giving him a soft smile. "Pack light. We can't afford to be weighed down."

He nodded. "So, only the sexy boxers. Got it. I won't be long. And maybe, once we get there, you can tell me who the hell we're hunting and why. Because there's no way you'd go rogue if this wasn't DEFCON one level shit."

He disappeared down the hallway, his words lingering in the air. He was right about one thing. She was walking a very fine line where the DEA was concerned — what her boss had sanctioned her to do — and if this didn't pan out the way she hoped, her career would be just another ghost in her past.

CHAPTER 3

"How the hell can it be this hot and yet the rain still chills you to the bone?" Booker glanced over at Callie, loving the way she smiled at him. God, she was beautiful.

Beautiful and smart and most likely the death of him because they were already standing outside the airport in San Juan, their stupidly light backpacks slung over their shoulders as he waited for his contact to text him where to pick up the Jeep.

Though, contact was an understatement. Charlie Cooper was so much more than a mere contact. Ex-military and some kind of weird mix between *Walter "Radar" O'Reilly* and *Templeton "Face" Peck,* the guy had this uncanny way of acquiring literally anything Booker could dream up. Just like now. A Jeep waiting somewhere in the parking lot with a chopper on standby at a small, out-of-the-way landing strip

Booker was sure most people probably didn't even know existed. Add to that, some reliable fire power, and they were armed for decent resistance. Not what Booker would have taken with him in the FCD, when getting shot down was always a possibility, but close.

Callie glanced around, her smile fading into a slight frown as she paused on certain people, silently measuring them up before continuing. Guys Booker suspected were gang members associated with the local drug cartel. Someone he assumed might recognize her if they looked hard enough.

Not that Booker thought any guy *could* forget Calliope Jensen. At least, he couldn't. Not since the day he'd met her, which explained why he was standing in the rain, in freaking Puerto Rico, with nothing more than his gut instincts that this was a mission worthy of his time. That Callie hadn't gone completely rogue.

Which had made explaining the impromptu assignment to Hank and Stone a bit awkward. Especially when all he could tell them was his location. That it was peripherally connected to the DEA, and that he hoped he could fill them in more, later. Of course, he'd offered to cover whatever expenses were the result of the op. That, if Hank or Stone thought this was just too insane, that Booker was more of a liability than an asset, they could oust his ass. But Hank had merely told him to get Charlie to liaise with him so he could ensure the man had access to whatever Booker needed. That they were there if he required backup.

He was still in shock from that. Sure, he'd sent Wyatt a quick text. More of a nine-one-one pre-warning that Booker might have to call on his buddy to come and save his and Callie's asses. That, if things went seriously sideways, Wyatt might be their only hope.

Wyatt had answered with nothing more than a stupid thumb's up emoji. What had probably been the fastest reply when Booker knew Wyatt and Kirby were likely on round three of their fuck-fest. But it meant Wyatt was onboard. Ready. Waiting. That, no matter the time or the cost, he'd been there.

Calliope nudged him, shifting closer as the rain picked up. "Any luck on unearthing where our ride is? Or are we just waiting for the rivers to flood so we can swim?"

"Very funny. Though, you, in a bikini…"

She slapped him on the chest, the inklings of a smile lifting her lips. "You're such an ass."

"I know." He held up his phone. "And Charlie just got back to me with where he left the Jeep, which means we won't have to swim, just yet."

She simply shrugged. "Mission isn't close to being over, so I wouldn't take that avenue off the table."

"I'd never take the chance of seeing you stripped down to your skivvies off the table, sweetheart." He grabbed her hand. "You ready? Anything or anyone I should be concerned about for the few minutes it'll take to reach the car?"

She rolled her shoulders, much like he did when his ghosts were pushing a bit too hard. "That obvious?"

"I might not know the details of what we're up against, yet, but I know *you*. So, any of those guys over by that muscle car a concern?"

She didn't glance at them, just nodded. "The two with the neck tats. They're pretty far away, but it'd be best if they didn't get a good look at my face."

"Roger. Though, with how sexy your ass is, I'm thinking they shouldn't get a good look at any part of you because I know I'd recognize the sway of your hips at any distance."

She froze for a second, giving him a questionable side eye before smiling as she moved in beside him, allowing him to keep her close. What he hoped gave the illusion of a couple strolling across the parking lot but provided him with a vantage point. The ability to jump in front of a threat or cover her if one of those assholes suddenly opened fire.

Reaching the Jeep without having to drop kick one of the gang members or take cover behind some of the other vehicles eased the pressure between his shoulder blades. A glimmer of hope that they'd at least get the mission started without one of them bleeding.

Callie slid into the passenger side, still glancing

over her shoulder. Those beautiful blue eyes searching. Whether it was to see if anyone had followed them or just out of habit, he wasn't sure. But one thing was certain — she'd definitely been on the wrong side of some sort of horrific incident. The kind of trauma that left scars that tugged at her sanity with every breath. Just like him and that damn crash he couldn't quite put behind him.

She pointed to his phone, still scanning the area. "I don't know where your friend, Charlie, is sending us, but we should try to avoid the major highways with toll stations and cameras. Just to be safe."

He started the vehicle, checked Charlie's directions, then joined the evening traffic. "Looks like he's got us going along the outskirts, so we should be okay."

Rain splattered across the windshield, the wipers barely keeping up. "When you said it rained a lot, you weren't joking."

She glanced at him, but he didn't miss the way she checked each mirror, first. "August is always a wild card. Is it going to be an issue for you? Flying in this stuff?"

"Not the greatest, but as long as our headwinds aren't too strong, and the fog isn't too thick, I can swing it. Assuming Charlie got me a decent ride, and this doesn't turn into a light and sound show."

Not that Booker had asked for anything fancy. Just a solid helicopter that could take a beating and keep on going. What he suspected might be a one-way trip with them trudging through the rainforest in order to get home. That inevitable "sideways" she'd mentioned.

Callie nodded, still scanning through the mirrors. "You're the expert. I trust your judgement."

"That's encouraging when I get the feeling trust isn't something you're giving away, right now." He spared her a quick glance. "Do I get to know what that's about? Why we're here, and if the DEA is at all okay with it? Are you even still working for them?"

She pursed her lips, looking incredibly sexy as she fiddled with a few strands of hair. What he assumed was her deciding on how much to tell him. Maybe what she *could* tell him.

She twisted enough to face him. "Honestly, I can't believe you agreed to come here without demanding to know everything, first."

He shrugged. "You needed a partner you could trust. If that's all you can tell me, then, that's enough."

"Damn, Booker..." She stared at him, eyes wide, mouth slightly open before she blew out a rough breath. "Before I start, I just want you to know... I *really* wanted to call you back. Pick up where we left off."

Booker wasn't sure if the warmth spreading through his chest was relief or arousal. Maybe an odd mixture of both, but it eased the prickling along his neck. Vanquished any lingering doubts because those few words told him everything he needed to know. "My delicate ego appreciates that because I was starting to wonder if I was the only one who was disappointed you passed out. That you regretted we even started anything."

She snorted. "I have a laundry list of regrets, baby, but you're not one of them. I just wanted you to know before..." She waved her hand in front of her.

"Baby?"

She paused, then laughed. "I can call you jackass or jerk like Wyatt if you prefer."

"Baby works for me. Now, back to... Shit!"

That's all the warning Booker could manage as headlights punched through the fog off to his right, barreling toward them from some two-bit side road barely wide enough to fit one car. He hit the gas, getting Callie's door clear before the SUV caught their rear bumper, spinning them clockwise as the other vehicle careened across the road, sliding sideways into the oncoming lanes.

Horns blared, one rusty old truck narrowing missing Booker's Jeep as the driver veered into their lane, shooting past them when Booker managed to maneuver them out of the spin — catch enough traction they shot forward. Water sprayed in every direction, the rear wheels fishtailing on the wet pavement before the Jeep straightened out. Started picking up speed.

He looked in the mirror, cursing when those

lights reappeared, quickly gaining on them. "Friends of yours?"

Callie glanced over her shoulder, shaking her head. "No way anyone got close enough to ID me."

"Too late to worry, now. I'll... Damn it."

"What?" Callie peered behind them, again. "Where the hell did they go?"

"I don't know, but I'm guessing they didn't disappear because this is over."

He scanned his mirrors, rolling down his window in the hopes of hearing an engine if they tried to parallel them, when the damn muscle car from the airport swung in from the left, spitting mud out behind it as it jumped the other lanes, then swerved in front of them.

Booker grabbed Callie's head, shoving it below the dash, then shifted gears, spinning the Jeep to the right when one of the gang bangers leaned out the window, shotgun pressed to his shoulder. The blast echoed around them as it shattered the rear driver's window, spraying glass across the interior.

Another spin, and Booker had the Jeep going in the opposite direction, wind and rain storming in through the broken window, those shards reflecting the lights cutting through the darkness. Tires squealed behind him, twin beams appearing in his rearview.

Callie popped up beside him, glancing at the road.

"Why are we going back? We'll get trapped in all the traffic if we head into the city."

"Just a short detour. I caught a glimpse of the road up by the bridge before I turned, and it looked as if the river flooded a bit. Everything's covered in water."

"Pretty sure the Jeep can handle it."

"I'm counting on that. Which means, we need to go faster."

"Faster? But…"

She inhaled as he increased his speed, forcing the bastards to follow before he reefed up on the parking brake. Took them into a full one-eighty spin.

The car whizzed past them, nearly colliding with a truck when they copied Booker's move. Sliding off onto the shoulder before finally finding their way back onto the road. They surged ahead, closing in on the Jeep, one of the assholes shooting at them, again.

The guy missed the rear window, sending a truck in the opposite lanes into the ditch when the buckshot took out a tire. Not that Booker had time to worry — stop and check if the driver was okay — with the muscle car gaining on them. He sped up just enough he rounded the corner first, blocked the flooded road from view before he slammed on the brakes — sent the car zooming past him.

It hit the pooling water going some insane speed, tires spinning uselessly on the slick pavement as it hydroplaned across the asphalt, slipping sideways from the force. A few more seconds, and it was heading for the guardrail, sending up sparks as the side panel scraped across the metal slats. Booker swerved in behind them, giving them an added push when it looked as if the driver might pull the vehicle back from the brink — regain control. Instead, the impact shot the car forward, catching one of the posts and jackknifing it up and over the edge. There was a harried moment of hang time — of the assholes all staring out the windows, mouths gaped open, eyes wide — before it hit the river below, all that dark churning water pulling it down.

Booker kept the Jeep moving, not even glancing at the water as he crossed the bridge, continuing along the highway. Callie checked their six, muttering to herself before easing against the seat, those gorgeous eyes focused on him.

He scanned the mirrors, half-expecting more cars to materialize out of the fog, only to sigh at the empty lane. He nodded at her. "Guess I was right."

She looked out the back, still cursing under her breath. "About what?"

"Your ass is way too fine for any man to forget."

"Not funny."

"But accurate." He took a deep breath, leveling his gaze at her. "So, this is where you start talking, sweetheart, and you don't stop until I know exactly what we're up against. And for the record, I don't care if it's legal. If you've gone rogue, and the DEA has a warrant out for you. If simply being seen with you gets my ass tossed in jail. I'm in, regardless. But I can't help keep us alive if I'm in the dark, so… lay it on me. And don't leave anything out, because there's no way this is over, and we don't have enough time or resources to adapt."

CHAPTER 4

CALLIE STARED AT BOOKER, surprised he hadn't simply pulled over and kicked her out. Left her to live or die by her own devices. She hadn't been joking. She still couldn't believe he'd agreed to accompany her without her putting it all on the line, first. Giving him the chance to back out.

He wouldn't. Not before, and definitely not after they were just attacked. But that didn't mean he liked being kept in the dark, as he'd phrased it, evident by the furrowed brow. Those sexy eyes that never stopped scanning their surroundings, before settling on her. Waiting.

She speared her fingers through her hair, praying he didn't notice the way her hand shook. Not that most guys would pick up on it. But Booker wasn't most guys. "It's—"

"Complicated?"

"Cliché, I know, but true."

"Good, because that's what I do best."

She sighed, knowing she had to tell him every-thing but unsure if she'd get through it without sinking into a flashback. And the last thing she wanted was to show him that side of her. The part she couldn't control. "The gist of it is, you weren't the only one who got called back to work, early. Have you heard anything about that scandal they've had in Florida with some DEA agents getting caught with their pants down in the Caribbean?"

"I heard rumblings about a grand jury."

"Well, apparently there was one contact who wasn't involved or outed, but he couldn't stay in case his identity had been compromised. But he was able to secure a new 'in' for another agent."

Booker glanced at her. "You? But, you're not even familiar with that cartel. I thought they kept agents curtailed to one location, so you knew the players? Made contacts you could trust."

"So did I. But my boss in Richmond, Keith Rogers, suggested they use me with the hopes that no one would know me when I hadn't worked an international case outside of Mexico. He claimed my experience with all the JSOC teams put me at the top of the list. Made it sound as if I was his only choice. Though, I'm sure the fact I was posing as some bigwig's girlfriend was part of the reason they chose me. Tits and ass, I suppose."

"Shit." He fidgeted on his seat, looking as if he was the one who wanted to crawl out of his skin. Or maybe punch one of those assholes they'd run off the road. "You didn't have to…"

"Have to, what?" She inhaled, swatting him across the chest. "Have sex with the asshole? Of course, not. I'm all for taking one for the team, Booker, but there are lines I won't cross. But, I did have to sell it. Hang off his arm like a freaking trophy. God, it was…"

"Demeaning?"

"And frankly, scary as shit. Staying at the guy's villa without any backup. Wondering if he was playing both sides. Just waiting for the perfect moment to out me in order to gain a better position in the family business. I haven't slept through the night for a year."

Booker reached over — took her hand in his and damn, it was so warm. Strong. He gave her fingers a squeeze. "I'm sorry. I can't imagine what you went through."

She shrugged, because what else could she do? "It all seemed worth it when I intercepted intel on a huge shipment of cocaine. I managed to contact my handler without getting shot — got a team assembled. We raided their crappy shack in the middle of the damn rainforest and seized nearly ten thousand kilograms of the stuff when an entire squad of mercenaries stormed out of the jungle. As if they'd been waiting for us to get inside — corner ourselves."

She ran her other hand through her hair, again, doing her best not to pull some of it out. "There were so many bullets flying, I couldn't even tell who was friendly and who was trying to kill me. We all got hit, and since armor-piercing rounds tend to leave a mark…"

She took a shaky breath, pushing at the images wavering in the dark. "I got lucky and had one of the metal wall panels fall on top of me. Guess they either missed me or didn't think it was worth moving when they came through searching for survivors."

"Getting shot then pinned was lucky?"

She ignored the pop gunfire sounding inside her head. The ghosted press of metal against her skin. "It's the only reason I'm still alive when nine other agents are dead."

He closed his eyes for a moment, his rough breath flaring his nostrils. As if he'd had to force it out without screaming. "They killed your entire team?"

"There's more."

Booker shook his head, giving her a hard stare. "They left you for dead. How can there be more?"

"I heard two men talking just before I passed out. One of them asked the other how much his fellow agents' lives were worth to him, and the asshole just laughed it off. Said he would have killed us for half of what he'd been paid."

"Shit." He gave her hand another squeeze. "Do you

know who set you up because you don't even have to ask, sweetheart, I'll just eliminate him for you."

She laid her other hand over their joined ones. "There's my hero. Unfortunately, no. The blood loss… I don't remember it clearly enough to place it, just that I was sure I knew the person. Either way, I'll recognize him."

He nodded, slowing down to take some small nondescript road off to their right. "Don't get me wrong, but isn't this a job for the DEA's special ops team? Don't they want this bastard caught?"

"Oh, I've tried. Spent the past month begging every senior officer I could track down to let me go back in with a team — find the fucker. But no one believes me. They all claim it was just my brain's way of making sense of the loss. That they did a thorough investigation, and they couldn't find any trace of a mole. Even Rogers insisted the remaining agents were clean. That I must have gotten this incident mixed up with something else. That he'd been keeping tabs on me the entire time, and we were simply in the wrong place at the wrong time and got caught in the middle of a drug gang war."

"But you don't believe that."

It hadn't been a question, and Callie simply shook her head. "If it was a gang war, why were we the only casualties?"

"So, this lack of faith from your agency is why you're going back alone."

"I'm not alone. I have you. And, before you ask…" She pulled out a burner cell from her pocket. "Yes, my current boss in Florida — Ted Higgins — is aware of what I'm doing. Well, mostly aware. I didn't tell him your name, or who you worked for, just that I knew someone who could get me back to that piece-of-shit shack on the down low. He's given me a very short leash. I'm supposed to observe and report, only. Keep him up-to-date of my whereabouts, then call him if I unearth any kind of evidence so he can send in a sanctioned team."

"But, you don't plan on standing down."

"Let's just say I'm leaving my options open."

"Sounds reasonable. So, why the big secrecy?"

She glanced away for a moment, staring out the window at the rain puddling on the road. "I guess I didn't want to give you any reason to say no."

"Why on earth would I say no?" He sighed when she looked back at him. "You were worried I wouldn't believe you, either."

"Even my office shrink thinks I'm crazy."

"That's because they don't know you like I do. If you say some dick agent set up your team, then we'll hunt the bastard down. Just, try to give me some warning before you go all *Black Widow* out there. So I don't look like a complete pansy when you do all the heavy lifting."

She was staring. She knew she was, most likely

with her mouth slightly open. Maybe some drool dripping down one side.

Callie wiped at her face, thankful it was dry then just shook her head because the guy was nuts. Certifiably crazy to trust her with nothing more than her word. Especially when no one else had even considered it. Which only made those lingering doubts she'd had seem foolish because Booker Hayes was definitely one of the last true warriors.

She nodded, turning to look out the window, again, hoping he hadn't noticed the tears pooling in her eyes. How close to the edge she was, and all because he'd given her the benefit of the doubt. Traveled a few thousand miles on the hopes the mission was justified.

That she wasn't playing him.

"I'll do my best."

"Good, because whatever crappy hanger Charlie's sending us to is just around that next bend. And I have a feeling we don't want to waste any time."

"Awwww, don't worry, Booker. I've got your back if more bad guys show up."

"Wasn't worried about you having my back. More that those bad guys will bring a bunch of friends with bigger guns."

"You're really something, you know that?"

"Funny, Kirby said the same damn thing at that bar, which I'm sure you overheard, since you were shadowing me. But I'm hoping your meaning is slightly different."

"I only got snippets. You were too vigilant to get that close. Are she and Wyatt still *keeping it casual?*"

He laughed. "Yup. I've been listening to Wyatt go on about how it's *nothing serious* for several years, now. I'm still hopeful they'll eventually figure it out."

"I think Kirby already has, she just needs to believe in it. From the few conversations we've had, I'm pretty sure I'm not the only one with trust issues. Which reminds me, in case I don't get a chance later... Thank you. You really didn't have to come."

"And miss a chance to show you how awesome I am? I don't think so, sweetheart." He smiled at her. "And you're welcome."

"Let's just hope you're half as awesome as I remember, because this isn't going to be easy."

"Easy's overrated."

"*Dying's* overrated, so let's try not to. Okay?"

"I already promised Wyatt I'd come back and tease him about how lovesick he is over Kirby, so dying isn't an option." He did that smoldering smile thing like in the movies. "Besides, you still owe me a date."

Callie leaned over, dragging one finger along his chest. "Help me nail this bastard, and I'll make you breakfast the next morning wearing nothing but your shirt."

Had his breathing sped up? Was his heart

pounding beneath her palm because of what she'd said or because of the adrenaline rush from the chase? She didn't know, didn't care because just *imagining* he wanted more was enough to get *her* heart racing. Made it hard to breathe inside the Jeep. As if that broken window was sucking all the air out instead of rushing it in.

"I like bacon. Lots of bacon."

She laughed as he rounded the bend, stopping in front of what looked like an old derelict hanger that would fall over from a strong breeze. Seeing some guy with shaggy hair and camouflage pants come marching out had her inhaling. Instinctively reaching for the gun she didn't have — couldn't bring without using her DEA credentials, which hadn't been part of the plan.

Booker chuckled, opening his door before stepping out — meeting her gaze across the hood. "Easy, sweetheart. Charlie's a bit of a lady's man, but he's not a threat. Besides, I have no doubt you'd easily kick his ass if needed."

Charlie shook his head, grabbing Booker's hand then yanking him in for a crushing bear hug once they'd reached the hanger. "God, damn, Hayes, you look as disheveled as the last time I saw you. Though, I gotta say… if this thing you've got going with Hank Patterson is half as profitable as I think it's gonna be, I might actually get to retire."

"You? Retire? I don't see it. And I hope you gave

Hank the friends and family discount, especially after that little trip I did for you last month."

Charlie coughed, then smiled. "Or course, I gave him a discount. We're practically brothers."

"In other words, you haven't sent him the final invoice and will add it on before I see the bill."

"It's like you know me." He motioned to the Jeep. "Christ, you've had my baby less than an hour, and she's already busted up. That might be a record, even for you."

"Not my fault people drive aggressively here."

"Right, so the shotgun holes?"

Booker simply grinned, placing his hand on the small of her back. "Charlie Cooper, this is Callie Jensen."

Charlie's eyes widened as he slid a side eye at Booker. "*This* is Special Agent Calliope Jensen? The one you flew around for over a year? Whose name you managed to bring up in almost every conversation? No wonder you didn't want to introduce me, you selfish prick. And honey, you're way too fine to be hanging with this jackass."

Booker placed a hand on his chest. "You know, I'd be insulted by that remark if it wasn't true. And before you get any wild ideas, she's way out of your league, too."

"Guess we'll have to see about that. But while we're at it, you could have told me this was for the DEA."

"It's not. At least, not officially. More peripheral-ly." Booker sighed at Charlie's arched brow. "It's complicated."

"When isn't it?" He crossed his arms over his chest. "I got those maps you asked for. You do know that part of the jungle is crawling with drug cartel and armed mercenaries, right?"

Callie snorted. "What part of the jungle isn't?"

Charlie chuckled. "I like her. Okay, I've got you set up with a Hughes 500. Booker already knows all this, but in case he doesn't share, I can tell you that this baby can take a beating and still see you safely home. Or keep you alive if you have to pack it in and roll down the side of a cliff. Though, I don't recom-mend trying that last one unless it's your only option. I've got a Sig and a Beretta in a lockbox in the back. Not the kind of fire power the cartel will carry, but I assume you won't get close enough to have to worry about that, right?"

Callie held up her hands. "Observe only, of course."

"Right. GPS doesn't always work that well up along that ridge, which means very spotty cell cover-age, too. That camera you wanted is also in the heli-copter. It should meet your needs, and then some. And I put in a couple of med kits. Just in case."

He motioned at the rain still pouring down. "You aren't seriously going to fly in this shit, are you, Booker? Because that would be insane, even for you."

"I've flown in worse."

"When you were with Flight Concepts. Had all those high-tech toys at your disposal. Your current ride has spotty GPS, a sticky throttle, and zero integrated navigation tools other than those maps I mentioned. We're talking old school with *old* being the key word."

"As long as she's sound,"

"Sound won't keep you flying if these downdrafts get any stronger"

Booker glanced at her, then the Jeep, looking as if he was weighing his options before he sighed. "Remember those shotgun holes? I think it'd be best if we got airborne before more assholes show up with assault rifles, this time."

Charlie waved him off. "I'm not completely oblivious to what's out there. I've got a few sensors along that road, and no one's followed you up it. Guaranteed."

"While that's comforting, I'd…" He paused, cocking his head to the side as he stared out at the rainy landing strip. Brow furrowed. His perfect mouth pursed into a tight line. "Do you hear that?"

Charlie huffed. "The distant roll of thunder? Yeah, which is what I'm trying to tell you. It's going to get a whole lot uglier out there before this storm passes, assuming it doesn't turn into something more tropical."

"It's not thunder…"

He peered into the darkness, tilting his head for a moment before he inhaled — twisting and taking them both to the ground before Callie could get a word out. Try to catch a glimpse of what he was looking at.

Not that she needed to look. Two seconds later, and the *whop whop whop* echoed through the air, a glint of something metallic shining in the sky from a distant fork of lightning. Another two seconds, and bullets were chewing up the ground, the muzzle flashes making the fog glow as dirt and grass shot into the air.

Callie had just enough time to see it fly past before Booker was yanking her to her feet — giving her a quick once-over. "Chopper, now."

"But it's still inside..." She let the words fade when he pointed at the machine, acknowledging that flying was his wheelhouse. Not hers.

Charlie ran over with them, his phone springing to life with pings and chirps. "Shit."

Booker merely shook his head, removing a few tie downs. "Let me guess... Those sensors are going off."

"You weren't joking about more guys with guns, were you."

Charlie hadn't asked, and Booker merely shrugged. "Open the doors as wide as possible then get your ass someplace they won't see you. I'm betting they'll leave as soon as we do." Booker handed Charlie a card. "This is Wyatt Bixby's number. If I don't call you in the next twenty-four hours to let you know we're both still breathing, call him and tell him to get his ass out of Kirby's bed and on a plane. And he's going to need everything you've got, buddy."

"I have another vehicle. You don't have to be bait, not to mention there's a thunderstorm heading this way."

"We'll be fine. And the thunderstorm is exactly what's going to get all our asses out of the fire. Stay safe. And, thanks… I owe you."

Booker hopped in the chopper, pushed in a few circuit breakers then started her up. No running through checks like Callie remembered from previous trips. No waiting for the dials to do whatever they normally did. All those times she'd watched him because he was so damn mesmerizing. So freaking handsome and strong. This was just a glance, then him firing up the machine. Getting it airborne in less than a minute.

He looked over to see if she was buckled, waited until Charlie had vanished, then picked up the helicopter and started for the open doors. Not that Callie thought they'd even fit because… Booker was halfway there, and she swore he was already chipping away at the walls. Sending bits of wood and dust swirling through the air.

Another few feet, and two guys appeared in front of them, guns at their hips. Faces hidden in the shadows. They lifted the rifles — muzzles aimed at the bubble — when Booker surged forward, picking up speed at some crazy rate. As if he'd kicked in a turbo boost.

The bastards got off a shot — pegged it through the bubble and into the instrument panel — before they were diving for cover. Booker nearly catching them both with the skid gear as he shot through the hanger doors, missing the frame by mere inches.

A tilt forward and a bank to the right, and they were screaming over the ground, quickly eating up the short stretch of open grass, a thicket of trees baring down on them. Booker kept going, keeping them a foot off the damn ground before angling them back. Shoving her into the seat as the chopper pitched up, the skid gear brushing a few leaves before they were clear. Nothing but rain and fog and utter darkness.

Booker glanced behind him, cursing, before looking her in the eyes. "Hold on, sweetheart. The ride's only just begun."

CHAPTER 5

Screwed.

No other way to put it. To soften the blow or downplay the situation. Just the two of them, alone in the chopper, royally fucked.

Booker checked to see if the other helicopter was dogging them, yet, then scanned the instruments, not that they were helping. The one shot those assholes had gotten off had taken out half the array, the remaining gauges just starting to normalize after his abrupt departure. Though, not hearing any alarms was a blessing, especially with the lack of a warmup followed by him pegging a few of the needles into the red as he'd barreled out of the hanger — raced across the ground before having her climb. Hard. But, desperate times...

He should have anticipated more men would follow this quickly. That the first car, which had disappeared, was still in the game. That they'd kept their lights off and used the fog to trail behind just enough to see Booker turn down the old road. That the bastards would call in reinforcements. Even if the assholes didn't know exactly where Booker had ventured, the road only led to one place.

God, he hoped Charlie was okay. That the men had left as soon as Booker had nearly plowed into the mercenaries. Because if he thought for a second that he might be the reason his buddy got killed...

Booker couldn't think that way. Charlie was resourceful. Had already vanished before the men had arrived at the hanger. And if Booker knew his buddy, the guy had several secure hiding spots already in place on the off-chance the wrong people came looking for him.

Not that Booker had time to worry when that helicopter from earlier appeared behind them, cutting across their path — a series of flashes preceding the barrage of bullets that filled the sky, a few ricocheting off the skid gear. What could result in a catastrophic incident if he didn't up his game. Be the guy he should have been all those months ago.

Callie glanced behind them, bracing one arm on the window when he banked it hard to her side, skimming across the trees then dipping into a small clearing that bordered on one of the rivers. He didn't wait to see if the other aircraft followed, simply cranked it over, then wound his way along the bank, everything rushing past in a dark blur. A few birds squawked then flew off, black streaks against the deep gray.

Thick fog rolled along the water, and he prayed it wasn't hiding anything he couldn't adapt to. That there weren't hidden wires or some kind of buoy. Maybe a boat just waiting for him to crash into it.

Having more bullets pelt the water as he dodged to his left eliminated any remaining doubts. Put everything into focus because he was not going to get shot down the one time Callie needed him to pull through.

Which meant, tilting the machine forward — gaining more speed. Really banking it around the corners, up and over a few bridges, then flaring the machine into a hover beneath one when it was apparent the other pilot was staying high. Hoping to anticipate Booker's moves.

He waited a few moments, grinning when more muzzle flashes lit up the fog farther along the river — where he would have been if he'd continued ahead. Which was his cue to move — shift the helicopter backwards before spinning midair and heading back along the water. He took a different branch, staying low, the fog swirling around him in twin eddies before he found a place to park along the riverbank. Not quite invisible, but with all the lights turned off and the fog curling in around them, it did the job.

They waited, minutes ticking by until more

thunder rumbled overhead, followed by a fork of lightning. Callie jumped, hands fisted so tightly together her knuckles were white. What Booker assumed was her fighting off reminders of that night. He just didn't know if it was his flying, being shot at, or the storm triggering the memories.

He reached over — gave her hand a squeeze. "You still with me, sweetheart?"

She huffed, cursing when another boom of thunder shook the chopper. "Kind of stuck with you. Though, I don't know how you can even see anything between the rain and the fog. The utter blackness. Are we staying here until the storm passes? Or…"

He sighed. "I know what I said before about it being an issue if the storm turned ugly like this, but we don't have the luxury of staying. And whether I like it or not, this storm is the best possible cover. Those assholes have guns mounted to the damn skid gear. We've got a forty-five and a nine-millimeter handgun. Not exactly what we need to go toe-to-toe with these jerks."

She nodded, but he didn't miss the tight press of her lips. How her breathing sped up, paused, then turned raspy. The lady was scared, but he knew she'd never admit it.

"I won't let you down, Callie. Promise."

She turned, looked over at him, and damn, she was glowing. Like that fire he'd claimed Kirby had lit inside of Wyatt. That same doe-eyed gaze that made

Booker's heart race. As if the stupid thing might pound right out of his chest.

Callie leaned over, getting her mouth dangerously close to his. "I know you'd never let me down. And if it were anyone else attempting to fly into the heart of a thunderstorm, I'd refuse. Would take my chances with the armed mercenaries, chopper or not. But with you..."

She shrugged, slowly shifting away. "You do what you think will keep us breathing, and I'll be there to back your decision if shit goes sideways."

"Let's try to save the really catastrophic stuff until *after* we find this shack. In the meantime, hold on. The ride isn't going to get any better."

She smiled, again. Gave him another shot of that light and what he swore was pride. Or maybe something purer. Deeper. What he suspected was the reason for his increased breath. The warmth spreading through his core.

He allowed himself one last moment to stare at her — memorize every feature — before he was scanning the skies. Lifting off into a hover once he felt confident the other pilot had bolted. A spin and a lift, and they were racing down the river, again, flying just high enough the upper half of the bubble was clear of the fog. Only wispy patches fading across his field of view instead of nothing but that eerie gray.

Thirty seconds in, and he was finally heading toward the rainforest. What looked like a giant black bullseye on the horizon. Until a flash of lightning illuminated the sky. Highlighted the thick canopy of trees. Sent what felt like an electric shock through the cockpit.

Callie muttered something under her breath, inhaling at the next strike. The one that was way too close. That had the hairs on Booker's arms standing on end. The errant strands of Callie's hair sticking straight out. He edged a bit closer to the treetops, hoping the lightning would strike something other than the damn chopper, when everything disappeared amidst a flash of white. A deafening roar echoing around them.

The helicopter shook, dropping several feet before Booker managed to counter the motion — not plow them into the trees. Not that his success lasted long. A few seconds later, and the instruments were smoking slightly, small wisps curling into the air as the rest of the panel went dead. The needles pegged in the green one moment, then reading zero the next.

He checked a few circuit breakers, but it was useless. "Looks like that hit fried everything left working."

Callie nodded. Too fast to be convincing, but at least she wasn't freaking out. No screaming or trying to grab his hand. Maybe opening the damn door because she was getting claustrophobic. Just a hint of white in her eyes. Those clenched fists. And her putting all her faith in him.

And he wasn't going to let her down.

"Hang in there. We're not too far from where we were heading. I'll find somewhere suitable and set her down. Check for any damage. See if we can push it a bit more or if we have to go on foot sooner than expected. Either way, we'll be fine."

God, he hoped they'd be fine. But, just to be safe, he gained some altitude. Gave himself a bit of a cushion in case they encountered a sudden down-draft. Sure, it risked them getting hit by lightning, again, but somehow that seemed better than drop-ping into the canopy of trees.

Having another flash streak past them had him reconsidering his options. That, maybe, they'd pushed their luck far enough. Should land while he still had control. And with the other helicopter nowhere in sight...

Hearing alarms blare through the cockpit a moment later had him shifting back to that fateful night. How he hadn't been able to save everyone. And without Wyatt and the others to have his back, Booker needed to pull a win out of his ass.

Which started with him getting out of his head and not overthinking everything. He didn't need the instruments. Hell, all he really needed were the years he'd spent behind the controls. All the senses he'd honed.

A deep breath, a roll of his shoulders, and he was all in. Was testing the give of the controls. Noting the slightly heavy feeling. How it took more pedal than usual to keep the bird straight and into wind. What was likely damage from the lightning strike. Or maybe some of the bullets had nicked the rotors. Left some holes that were starting to become an issue.

He took a chance and banked her over, searching for somewhere to land that wouldn't leave them vulnerable. A hole in the trees he could land in without crashing or leaving them with no other option but to walk out. Not that he was confident they'd be able to fly the machine, again. But damaged or not — wise or not — he wanted to leave that door open. Even if they only got a few more miles out of her, it might save their lives.

Seeing an old dirt road open off to their right was exactly what he needed. Not a lot of room, but enough he could follow it along the mountain if needed. Use it as a runway if the hydraulics acted up, or if he required the extra distance to gain some altitude later. Their Hail Mary once Callie had gotten the proof she needed.

Setting it down as more lightning lit up the forest took a bit of finessing. Fighting the sudden gust of wind as the rain picked up — swallowed all the light once the glow from the flash faded. Left nothing but utter darkness in its wake. The tall trees eating up any other hint of gray on the horizon. But, with some steady hands and a healthy dose of luck, he managed to put the bird safely on the twin tracks — kept the rotors from hacking any of the trees. What would have ruined that last-ditch-option he'd been hoping to save.

Callie released a shaky breath as he spooled down the engine and waited for everything to shut off. She didn't speak, just stared at him, eyes wide. Those kissable lips pursed together.

He frowned, leaning over to her side. "Are you okay? You didn't get hit, did you?"

He started searching for wounds when she palmed his jaw — waited for him to look up at her. "I'm fine, I'm just... Remind me to thank you once this is all over."

"Thank me for what? Not crashing? Because that's kinda my job."

"For being more than just a guy I can trust. You..."

She closed the distance — kissed him. Not the way they'd kissed that night before everything had changed. This was soft. Sensual. But damn, it spiked his heart rate even more than if she'd tangled her tongue with his. Had him fighting not to fist her hair — hold the back of her head and keep her there. Mouths pressed against each other. Nothing but the fog and the rain and the darkness surrounding them.

But now wasn't the time. Or the place.

She eased back. Swallowed. Though, he didn't miss how it seemed to take effort. That maybe she was fighting some of the same emotions that welled inside of him. How he wanted to live because she'd given him a glimpse of what life could be like if he had the balls to seize it.

He did his best to swallow, too. Nearly choked when her eyes darted to his mouth, again, but he managed not to die right there in the chopper.

Callie smiled, then brushed her thumb across his lip. "You sure you're still up for this?"

He scoffed. "Do you really think I'd let you go alone?"

"No, but... It seemed only right to offer you an out when I hadn't really given you one to begin with."

"Don't need an out. Just whatever Charlie left for us in the back because as crazy as it might sound, getting this far was the easy part. Now... now the true adventure begins. So, let's saddle up, and catch the son of a bitch who set you up."

CHAPTER 6

SPEECHLESS. A first for Callie, but hearing Booker say he didn't need an out — that he just needed a weapon and to help her nail the double agent who'd killed her team and left her for dead — took her breath away. They'd just been chased by armed mercenaries. He should be tossing her ass out, not gearing up. Hell, they hadn't even really slept together — made any kind of promises. Just the start of something magical that had ended early because Booker wasn't the kind of guy to ever take advantage of a situation.

Which only made all the heat swirling around inside her burn hotter. To the point she was surprised she wasn't sending off little bolts of lightning. Just like the storm. Arcs from her to him. That law of attraction she vaguely remembered from school. And there was no denying she was attracted to Booker Hayes.

Booker grinned, that smile igniting another round of sparks beneath her skin. "What are the coordinates for that shack, again?"

Callie shook herself from her thoughts, focusing on Booker. He had one of the maps spread out in front of him, his phone illuminating the small space.

She reached into her pocket, then handed him the paper. "It's just inside El Yunque, but I know that the crappy dirt road up that way has been blocked off. They say it's for safety reasons — something about the road being unstable from the hurricane that destroyed half the island. But the cartel has enough officers in their pocket they can pretty much get anything cordoned off. And it limits who can sneak up on them."

Booker nodded, quickly finding the spot on the map. "It's not as close as we would have liked, but it looks like there's a parallel trail. Probably overgrown and slower, but I doubt we want to amble up the main road when we have no idea if those assholes chasing us already alerted their buddies you were coming back for another round."

"I still don't know how they recognized me for the two seconds they might have seen my face, especially when we were pretty far away."

He just laughed. "Your ass speaks for itself."

"You're such a jerk."

"I know." He glanced out the window, sighing at another round of lightning streaking across the sky.

"I hope you've got a decent rain jacket in that backpack."

"It's one of the only things I brought. You?"

"Yup, along with those sexy boxers I mentioned. Ready? As much as I'd like to stay here and wait it out, I think it's best if we keep moving. Hopefully stay a few steps ahead of your welcoming committee."

"You got the route memorized? Or are you getting sloppy?"

Booker merely arched his brow. "Are you seriously questioning my skill as a tracker? That hurts, sweetheart."

"Charlie said he packed a couple of med kits. I can get a Band-Aid for you, if it'll help."

"Brat. And we should bring one along. Just to be safe. You want the Sig or the Beretta?"

"Beretta. I assume you can handle the forty-five?"

"First, my tracking skills, and now my marksmanship? You're killing me. I've got two mini smoke canisters, too. Though, if we have to use them, it'll mean things are pretty desperate."

He opened the door, holding it against the gusting wind, then made his way to the back. A quick scrounge in the boxes Charlie had left, and he had their weapons, flashlights, and a med kit out. Was packing some stuff into his bag before handing her a light, her gun, and a few extra mags. Once she'd secured the items, he passed her some rain gear then slipped on his.

He placed the extra med kit in the lockbox, stuffed it back into the smuggling compartment, then signaled for her to wait before heading to the rear of the helicopter. She was just about to join him — see if he'd somehow gotten lost or was fighting off tangoes she hadn't noticed — when he opened her door.

He motioned to the back. "The tail rotor's got a bit of damage, along with some holes in the fuselage. A few nicks on the main rotor blades, too. Nothing catastrophic, but definitely not in our favor. If needed, I could get her airborne, again."

Callie sighed, wondering how everything had gone for shit so quickly. Before they'd even reached the shack — possibly confronted the asshole who'd set her up. "But it's not ideal."

"Dying's not ideal, so... We'll do whatever is necessary to see we stay breathing. If that means I milk this baby for all she's got before putting us down somewhere else, preferably closer to civilization and possible backup, then, so be it. Ready?"

And there it was. That never-say-die attitude shining through. Making those mesmerizing eyes of his glow despite the lack of any true light. As if it was coming from inside him.

She accepted his hand, inhaling when he pulled her against him, his other hand tracing a line down her back — pausing on the top of her ass. He didn't speak, just stared for a few heartbeats before slowly backing up and checking the map as he took a deep breath.

Was he as disappointed as she was that he hadn't kissed her? Because her pulse was tapping wildly beneath her skin. That burning feeling practically nuclear, now. She forced herself to swallow, to shove everything down that wasn't connected to hiking through the storm — finding proof she wasn't crazy. That she hadn't imagined some double agent casually brushing off her entire team being slaughtered.

That she was still sane. Still the agent she'd always been.

Booker glanced over at her, looking as if he was reading her thoughts, again, before pointing to a small gap in the trees. "The trail starts there then winds through the trees and brush. Any nasty snakes or spiders I should be concerned about?"

"Just one. The Puerto Rican Racer. It won't kill you, but it'll make you regret getting bitten. Damn thing leaves you numb for nearly a month. Not a fun time."

"Sounds like you've had the misfortune of encountering one."

"Let's just say my time here didn't leave me with many happy memories."

The jerk winked, giving her ass an obvious once-over. "Maybe we can change that after we're done."

Callie closed the distance between them, tracing

her finger along his pecs like she'd done in the car. "It'll take more than some mind-blowing sex to block out the past year, but I'm game to try if you are."

Booker coughed, pounding on his chest when it seemed as if he was choking, then shook his head as he clicked on his flashlight. "You're as dangerous as ever. And mind-blowing is way too mild for how it'll be if we ever get the chance to finish what we started. You should shoot your boss a quick text. Let him know we're heading to that shack. Hope the damn thing goes through because Charlie wasn't kidding about the sketchy service. I'll hit him up, too. Let the big jerk know we haven't died, yet. Tell me if you hear any assholes coming up from behind."

He struck off, leaving her standing there for a moment as she tried to push down the riotous leap of her heart. The one that wanted to see exactly how hot they might be together. How he'd surpass her expectations. Then, she was typing out a few words to her boss before jogging to catch up, falling in behind him as he picked his way along the over-grown trail, pausing periodically to move a branch out of the way or avoid what looked like knee-deep mud.

It took nearly four hours to traipse their way up the winding trail, along the ridge, then down the backside of the mountain, but it was worth it when that damn shack materialized out of the forest. Trees and brush one moment, that metal hut standing out like a dark scar the next. Not that it was easy to spot with the rain falling like a curtain around them. More of that eerie fog weaving through the trees. What might be the start of something more dangerous — that tropical storm Charlie had warned them about.

But she suspected it hadn't been an accident or luck that they'd come out of the thick forest right at the edge of the clearing. That Booker was far more than just a skilled pilot. Which made sense. Not that there was a lot of intel on exactly what the Flight Concepts Division did, but one thing was clear. The pilots underwent the same extreme training as the guys they flew in. Were able to pilot damn near any kind of machine, both domestic and foreign, and were apparently just as fearless because looking at him, there was no doubt he was primed and ready for a fight. Would stand between her and a dozen mercenaries without blinking, just like in the chopper when they'd been chased.

Nothing but calm, determined grace under pressure.

Booker doused his light as he stopped behind a collection of trees, studying the building until she half-wondered if he'd fallen asleep, before he sighed and looked over at her. "It's impossible to tell if there are any assholes in that shack, let alone how many."

He checked his gun, a small twitch of his mouth the only indication he was at all on edge. "Assuming we get inside without this turning into a full-scale battle, what are your intentions? Because I need to know if we're really just gathering intel or if I should be palming a knife in my other hand."

She pursed her lips, that burner cell in her pocket a not-so-subtle reminder of what she had been sanctioned to do. How far her boss was willing to let her venture before she'd crossed a line.

She stared at the cabin, pushing against the images gnawing away at the barriers she'd erected. What she'd needed to stay sane. The cartel had obviously rebuilt the shack. Erased any evidence that her colleagues had died. That the land was tainted. Cursed, really. And with the rain pouring down...

It was virtually the same scenario as that fateful night. Storm brewing. What looked like the perfect chance to barge in and round up the assholes manning the office. Pray the bastard who'd set her up was there. But with how poorly the first raid had turned out, she wasn't sure what she wanted to do.

Booker squeezed her shoulder, giving her a guarded smile. "I recognize that look, sweetheart. Either you're here for justice of revenge. Doubtful we'll get both, so... decide."

She cocked her head to the side, trying to determine if he'd stay if all she really wanted was revenge, before sighing. "And you'd be okay if I said all I really wanted to do was cap the bastard who'd left me bleeding in the mud?"

The muscle in Booker's temple jumped as he clenched his jaw, his gaze sliding to the shack then back. "I said I'd have your back, and that's a given, regardless of what happens in there. But it's not whether I can live with you capping this guy. The question is... Can you? Because there's a fine line between wanting revenge and exacting it. And you need to be a thousand percent sure you can still look at yourself in the mirror before you start writing checks your sense of honor can't cash."

Well, crap.

Callie glanced over at the building, wishing Booker hadn't voiced what had been racing through her head since she'd made the impromptu trip to West Yellowstone — enlisted the help of the only man she trusted with more than just her life.

And he'd done exactly what she'd known he would do and called her on it.

She sucked at her bottom lip, wanting to say she could march in there and shoot the creep in the head. Sleep like a baby for the rest of her life, but the lie wouldn't form on her tongue.

Instead, she released a shaky breath — met Booker's expectant gaze. "I want him to pay, but I can't kill someone without justification. That's not who I am."

Booker's hand slid down her back, resting on her ass, again. "That's my girl. Okay, we go in. You photograph everything in sight, grab whatever we can take with us, then we bug out. Call your boss once we're clear and let the DEA do the rest. Agreed?"

She nodded because if she said yes, it meant she'd taken the high road, and she hated taking the high road.

He laughed. "I know that look, too, and I get it. But sometimes, doing what's right — what you can live with — isn't as simple as doing what's easy. What you think will soothe that burning beneath your skin. But, I'll do my best to make it up to you, later."

He gave her a nudge. "Lead the way. I've got your six. And if our friends start shooting…"

All bets were off, which eased the jumpy feeling in her gut. Had her laser focused because she knew as sure as the storm would get worse before it got better, that this night wouldn't end without more bullets flying their way. And that was the one scenario where she might just get both wishes. The moral high ground she needed to get her revenge without losing her soul.

Making it to the side of the crappy shack without anyone walking out or yelling at them was a blessing. Especially after all they'd been through to get this far. How she'd half-expected the entire cartel family to be standing in a circle around the building, waiting for her to show up.

Having Booker pick the lock in ten seconds flat was unexpected. She'd arched a brow, but he'd merely shrugged, muttering something about growing up in foster care — that he'd learned early how to escape a bad situation, which only made her acutely aware that there was so much she didn't know about him. Was itching to find out.

Which meant making it out of the rainforest alive.

Callie followed Booker inside, sticking to the shadows as he picked his way across the room, heading for the office on the far side at the top of a set of rusted metal stairs. He didn't talk, just made his way to the steps, listened for a few moments, then started up. Boots barely making a sound.

Christ, had he done more than just pilot for special forces? Because the guy seemed as highly skilled as any black ops soldier she'd worked with in her various JSOC teams. More so because Booker's abilities extended far beyond the ordinary. Were the only reason they were both still breathing.

Questions she could ask him later, after they'd gotten some scrap of proof she wasn't crazy. That she hadn't dragged him all the way to Puerto Rico because of some harebrained memory that was nothing more than the product of blood loss and a healthy dose of guilt.

Booker held up his fist, pressing his ear to the door before trying it. Having the handle turn and the door swing open from nothing more than a push of his hand was a surprise. One she wasn't sure was in their favor when it could be a trap. A way to trick them into the room then have a dozen mercenaries open fire.

Or maybe the creep she was after would use a drone — get a kick out of the fact the DEA's own weapon had finally killed her. Unlikely, seeing as the winds had picked up in the short time they'd been inside. Sounded as if the walls might give way at any second, just like the night of the raid. But Callie wouldn't rule it out. Not with Booker's life on the line.

Though, if Booker worried they were being set up, he didn't show it. Seemed completely at ease as he pulled out his mag light — concentrated the beam on the desk. Another quick twist of the tools he'd brought along, and he had the drawers open and the files stacked on the top.

He motioned to them. "Start clicking, sweetheart, and be quick. I have a very bad feeling we're already out of time."

"You think it's a setup?"

"I think we've gotten extremely lucky, so far."

"Pretty sure us still being alive has nothing to do with luck and everything to do with you, but I'll be quick."

She started working her way through the stack, taking photographs of everything. Ledger sheets. Drug shipments. Images of the key players, and any surveillance they'd recorded. The kind of intel she would have thought would be locked away in a safe.

Or maybe stored on a thumb drive, not stashed in a desk. But, with little in the way of technology this deep in the forest, it made sense the cartel kept track of everything on paper.

Still…

Booker stayed close, making regular trips to the door to watch for men. Moving like a damn wraith because Callie didn't hear anything other than the soft rustle of paper as she flipped pages, stopping when she reached a series of photos.

"Well, fuck."

She looked over her shoulder as Booker's voice whispered in her ear. Not that she was surprised because… Her face was plastered all over the images. All at weird angles, but there was no denying it was her. At the villa. In the street. One of her on her cell when she'd been reporting to her handler. What she thought had been on the down low, only she'd been tailed.

Booker grabbed some of the photos. "This is more than enough proof you were setup, unless the cartel has a damn drone."

She whipped her head down, groaning when she realized he was right. That the weird angles were the result of some jagoff manipulating a zoom camera from up high.

He moved some of the photos, picking up a small recorder before activating it. Groaning when her voice sounded over the speakers. "Jesus, Callie.

They're splicing what I assume are wire taps together — making it sound as if you're the mole. Hear those rough patches, where the words overlap? That's where they haven't quite made it flow together."

She nodded, ice slicing through her veins at some of the phrases. "Christ, that's from my secure connection to my handler. How did they get that?"

"Easy, your mole is someone high up. Probably the last person you'd expect. You sure this Higgins guy can be trusted?"

"I don't know. I think so. He's never given me any reason to question him." She closed her eyes. "It really was my fault. I should have known I was being watched. Taped. I should have—"

"No way you could know they were watching you from a fucking drone. Or had people hacking into secure footage. Maybe some blue uniforms on the payroll. But, they obviously knew you were a plant from the start, and they were setting you up to take the fall, only, you didn't die. We need to go. Now."

Booker stuffed the camera, recorder and half the photos into his bag, then flicked off his flashlight, grabbed her hand, and headed for the door. He barely paused before clearing the platform then heading down the stairs.

Less than thirty seconds, and they were closing in on the exit — were moving fast — when the handle rattled. Booker changed direction mid-stride, dragging her behind a couple of crates on the opposite side of the room. What was barely enough cover to hide one of them, let alone two. But he managed to squeeze in behind her — what she prayed would appear as more shadows. Obviously refusing to separate when he could have darted behind more cover farther over. But the man she knew wouldn't leave her. Period.

Hearing boots tap across the floor had her holding her breath. Silently willing the creep to keep moving. Head up to the office so they could sneak out the door. Then the guy chuckled, and she knew they were busted. That it had either been a trap like she'd been worried about, or someone had noticed the flashlight beam bouncing around the office through one of the grimy windows.

Another laugh, then the boots stopped halfway across the floor as a dim light brightened the far side of the room. "I know you're in here, Calliope, so... just come on out. We need to talk."

Callie wasn't sure what had her inhaling. That the bastard knew she was there or that she recognized his voice. The same one she'd heard before passing out. That she'd spent over a decade listening to in her home office. The one man she'd looked up to since joining the DEA. Was that why he'd kept tabs on her all this time? Had he sent her undercover knowing he was going to have her and her entire team eventually killed? Had he lost any sleep over it?

Booker squeezed her hand, shaking his head as he

held up his gun. But she wasn't going to risk being the reason he died. Not when she suspected this wouldn't be a quick takedown. That the traitorous bastard wanted to draw it out. Maybe try to turn her. That he'd have a dozen men waiting outside as backup.

She grabbed the burner cell out of her pocket, and gave to Booker — mouthed for him to hide it. Then she motioned for him to stay, hoping he got the message because they only had one chance at making it out of the room still breathing, and it all came down to him.

One deep breath then she stood, calmly walking out from the shadows. Smiling when the guy turned and stared at her. Gun still sitting in the holster at his chest. Eyes fixed on her.

She moved a few feet away, blocking any view of Booker hiding behind the crates, then crossed her arms over her chest. "Hello, Keith. And yeah, we should probably talk."

CHAPTER 7

KEITH?

Well, shit.

While Booker didn't know everyone in high-ranking positions within the various agencies, he knew the main players. The men and women in charge, and the only Keith he knew in a power position within the DEA was Callie's previous boss, Keith Rogers. The one she'd told Booker had suggested her for the undercover position, claiming she had the most experience. Was the only choice.

Which was fucking code for her being too good to be left in the game. Expendable because if the guy was behind the operation down here, he'd definitely want to get rid of anyone who might figure it out. And even with Callie being a few thousand miles away, Booker knew she was smart enough — determined enough — to unravel any mystery given the chance. Especially if agents started dying.

He grabbed his phone and clicked on the voice memo app. He wasn't sure how clear everything would be, but he wasn't going to miss an opportunity to get the bastard talking on tape. Then Booker shifted over until he was behind the far side of the boxes, leaning out just enough to get an idea of where they were standing. Judge if this Keith, asshole, had anyone else backing him up. Seeing a shadow by the door confirmed there was at least one other player standing in the wings. Probably waiting for Keith to give him a signal — maybe have the other guy do the actual shooting, because there was no doubt in Booker's mind *someone* would start shooting.

Which was why Calliope had confronted the bastard. The lady was honorable to a fault, and it only made him fall a bit harder. Realize that she was the reason he'd been holding out on fully moving on with his life. He'd been hoping she'd find him.

Booker wasn't sure if the two jackasses knew he was there or if they assumed she'd come alone. That her pilot was waiting by the machine. He hoped it was the later. That, part of her reason for confronting them was to give him an edge. If they already knew he'd accompanied her...

Callie hitched out a hip, looking dangerously calm, considering she was facing down the man who'd already tried to kill her. Had eliminated her team. "It all makes sense, now. Why you were so eager to send me here. Why my brain didn't want to remember your voice. Why you insisted I'd imagined an agent behind everything. Though, I have to say, I'm disappointed."

She took a small step forward. It didn't look like much, but it opened up Booker's sight line. Gave him a better chance at capping both guys if needed. "If you wanted me dead, you should have had the balls to do it, yourself."

Booker had to give Keith credit. The guy didn't seem fazed. Just stood there, smirking. Like he knew some big secret.

Keith shrugged. "I prefer not to kill people I care about. And I do care about you, Callie."

"Just not enough to keep me alive."

The guy sighed, as if it had been hard to put her on some shit list. "You're smart. And your record speaks for itself. I knew it was only a matter of time before Washington reassigned you. Had you look into the epic shitstorm my cohort created down here, especially if other agents started dropping. And there was no way you wouldn't put all the pieces together — uncover my involvement. I just couldn't let that happen."

He took a couple of steps to the right, glancing where Booker had been hiding a few minutes earlier before focusing on Callie. And Booker knew that the asshole was looking for him. That he'd either spotted them coming in or had already checked out the chopper — found it empty. Which meant Booker needed to devise a plan.

He held firm, waiting until Keith had finished scanning the room, again, before taking a chance and sliding over to the next set of crates. It wasn't far, just a few feet, but it meant he only had the shadows to cover him for the two seconds he was scooting. Using every trick he'd learned in the service to stay hidden. Not make a sound as his boots slid across the old floor.

Making it there without Keith opening fire or his buddy charging across the room gave Booker a glimmer of hope. That maybe he'd be able to get Callie out without her getting shot. Killed. Of course, they might not both make it, but as long as she stayed alive, he could live with the fallout.

Even if living with it only lasted a second.

Keith tilted his head, scouring the room one more time before shrugging. "Which meant changing my tactics and getting ahead of the situation. You were the natural solution. I knew if there was someone above reproach assigned to the undercover job, no one would question it when that person's team got caught in what appeared to be a gang war. Wrong place, wrong time. It was unfortunate you were the only one who fit the bill."

Callie didn't react. Didn't give any indication she

was worried Keith was constantly searching the shadows. She just stood her ground. Calm. Strangely detached. "I'm sure it really tore you up, inside. Though, I assume having the board wiped clean gave you some solace."

"Hard to prove there's a mole without any evidence. Speaking of which…" He waved his fingers at her. "I'll take whatever you stole from the office."

She laughed, shifting again and damn, she had good instincts. Had opened up Booker's new sight lines as if she'd anticipated his strategy. Knew exactly where he was crouched. "As you can see, there isn't anywhere to hide anything in this outfit."

"Please, cell phones are extremely small, these days."

"Do you really think I'd be stupid enough to bring a phone in here when I know it can be tracked, even if it's off?" She nodded toward the side of the shack. "I tossed the camera out the window, just to be safe. I was gonna pick it up on the way out. But I'm sure that guy standing over in the shadows can find it, if he really tries. Or the other half a dozen lackies you have waiting outside."

Keith glanced over his shoulder, then back to her, that stupid grin crinkling the corners of his eyes. "See? You're a bit too good for my well-being. And I know you took more than just photos. I want the recorder, too. And I have no doubts you could squeeze it into those pants, wet or not."

She sighed, raised her hands, then slowly spun, pausing with her back to Keith as her gaze found his, held for a second, before she turned, again. Focused on Keith. "Nothing underneath these clothes but skin. And you're crazy if you think you can just cap me, here, and not have it turn into another international incident. My new boss knows where I am. What I'm doing. There's no way he'll believe I just stumbled upon another gang war when I've already told him I know there's a mole."

"You're putting a lot of faith in Ted Higgins. What do you even know about the man? You've only been part of his office for a year."

"Apparently time isn't the best judge of character because I've known you for damn near fifteen, and you still turned out to be a lying son of a bitch." She nodded at the creep still standing in the doorway, lowering her hand until it was within reach of her gun. "Are we just going to stand here, Keith, or are we going to get this party started?"

"I'm not going to kill you. You're worth more to me alive."

"Since when?"

"Since you survived my first attempt. It's like you said... Killing you now would raise suspicions. Have Higgins asking too many uncomfortable questions. But I would like to know where your partner is?"

"What partner?"

"Don't play coy with me, Calliope. I've been on to

you since the airport. I know about your rendezvous at that air strip, and your rather impressive escape in that helicopter. Mad skills, I'm told. The funny thing is, you're not a pilot."

"Are you sure about that? A lot can happen in a year."

"Oh, so you learned to fly while you were entertaining drug cartel? I know you're not alone."

Callie shrugged, as if it wasn't a big deal. "He's waiting at the chopper."

"I highly doubt that."

"I needed a pilot. Nothing more." She cocked her head over, shaking out her hand in what Booker assumed was her way of getting ready to draw. "I doubt it'll come as a surprise that I'm not very trusting these days."

Keith didn't move, just stood there, occasionally scanning the shadows. "Or maybe you enlisted the help of someone you already trust. Someone you're confident can't be bought. I can think of a few of your contacts who might have the skill to fly a chopper in this weather and not plow it into a tree. But one who has the moves to evade another helicopter at the same time, who's also skilled enough to back you up? Who'd jump on a plane without hesitation and from nothing more than your word? That's a limited list. In fact, only one name springs to mind, and *that guy* wouldn't let you out of his sight. Too much honor. Isn't that right, Captain Hayes?"

Showtime.

Booker shut down the app, tucking his phone in his pocket. He grabbed one of the mini smoke canisters, hooking the pin around his thumb before standing. No hiding or hesitating. He simply stood then moved out, hands out to either side — his Sig within reach at his waist. "It's just Booker, now. I'm retired."

Keith smiled. "You're going to be permanently retired unless you do exactly what I say, because unlike Calliope, you don't have to be part of the plan."

"That would be a shame. I was just starting to put it all together."

Keith pointed to Booker's shoulder. "Throw me the bag, or I'll risk the repercussions and just kill you both, now. And don't bother going for your gun, or my associate will ensure you're both dead before Callie can even draw."

"Well, when you ask so nicely..."

He made a point of easing the pack off his shoulder, removing the pin from the grenade as he went, before tossing them both toward Keith. The canister bounced across the floor, each hit sending a small shrill through the air. Keith gasped, diving out of the way as Booker drew his gun — shattering the light before catching the guy racing in from the door. Sending him tumbling backwards just as Callie laid down more cover rounds. Buying Booker enough time to grab her and the bag then make a run for the window behind them.

Two steps, and he had the glass already cracked — was lining up the best route. A few more, and he was hoisting Callie into his arms as he launched them at the window, using his shoulder to take the brunt of the force as they crashed through, landing in the mud with a dull thud.

He rolled, pulling her with him when he stumbled to his feet. She slipped, nearly taking them both back down before she managed to catch her balance — head for the trees. Shots erupted behind them, pelting the ground as they dove for cover, Callie rising up beside him and laying down more rounds. Sending what looked like a damn squad of men ducking behind the building.

No way they'd make it to the chopper without getting shot. Which meant going with Place B. Or maybe it was C. He pointed to a break in the trees, then took her position, going through a full mag while she made a dash for the trail — returning fire when he hoofed it after her.

He shoved her ahead of him, trying to block any shot as they raced along the muddy path, pushing through the overgrowth without stopping. The wind whipped branches in their face, more lightning and thunder crashing around them. That tropical storm Charlie had been concerned about rolling in.

Not that they had time to worry about the weather with a dozen mercenaries following behind them. Five minutes in, and the assholes were gaining. Getting off the occasional shot. Not that Callie wasn't sprinting like the wind. But between the gusting rain and the mud, it was hard to get any traction, both of them slipping sideways every other step. Not to mention how hard it was to navigate the trail in the dark. What was likely the other men's advantage. Knowing the terrain. Where all the twisting side trails led to instead of blinding barreling through the undergrowth like a couple of gorillas.

Booker was working on another plan. On how to send Callie off in one direction while he flanked around — killed as many as he could in order to give her a fighting chance — when she screamed as she dropped out of sight. Literally several paces ahead of him one second, nothing but inky forest the next.

He slid to a halt, cursing the line of mud snaking its way down an embankment where the edge had given way, taking Calliope with it. What looked like one hell of a ride with god knew what at the bottom. Not to mention that the initial fall, alone, could have injured her, leaving her in a heap at the bottom.

Now Booker understood why Wyatt was always telling him how adapting was a bitch. Sure, Booker had often altered his plans while flying, but he'd always had control. Had known the risks, the possible outcomes, and had acted accordingly. This...

This was just a giant black hole.

Not that it made a difference. Two deep breaths, then he was down on his ass, holstering his weapon then giving a shove to get himself going. A few seconds in, and he was flying down the mud, trying to use his upper body to steer — avoid crashing into trees and rocks. He'd traveled for what felt like a few hundred feet when the ground dropped out from beneath him. Solid one second, nothing but air the next. Him hanging for a moment, the rain and wind pausing before he was rushing toward the emptiness.

Hitting water instead of a bunch of rocks was the one lucky break he'd caught. Had him kicking his feet until he broke through the surface, gasping in a much-needed breath. Just like that night of the crash. Water spraying across his face. Nothing but darkness and the unrelenting current trying to drag him down. He squinted to see if Callie was ahead of him, but it was useless, the eerie gray blending in with the churning water.

A sound. Off to his left. Not much. More of a hushed whimper, but he managed to focus on the area — spot Callie's head bobbing in the water.

That's all Booker needed to strike off. He wasn't the accomplished swimmer Wyatt was, but Booker could hold his own. Wyatt had seen to that. Had been borderline sadistic in ensuring Booker was as close as possible to being SEAL proficient in the water without actually undergoing BUD/S. Which meant Booker would have to thank the jerk if he actually made it out of this damn mission in one piece.

Took him longer than he'd anticipated to reach her, fighting that current the whole way. Seeing blood dripping down her face nearly unhinged him. Had him upping his pace — putting every last ounce of strength into each stroke. Cutting through the white-tipped waves as quickly as possible. Having her go under while he was still several feet away flipped a switch in his head. Or maybe it was his heart. Either way, it gave him an added boost. Had him diving under — eyes wide, trying to see anything in the murky depths.

Catching her hand just before his air ran out was his second lucky break. The best one so far because it meant he hadn't lost her. Hadn't broken his promise. That he could still be the man she needed him to be.

Callie was spiting up water as they crested the surface, the current still pulling them along. The bank rushing past in a dark blur. He wrapped his arm under hers and around her chest — just like Wyatt had done to him. Used the connection to steady his nerves.

This was way outside his wheelhouse. Flying in a thunderstorm had been familiar. Comforting, really. The kind of threat he'd dealt with for the past fifteen years. What he was good at. Exceptional, if he was being honest. Dealing with armed mercenaries had been a bit more of a stretch. Not something he'd done a lot of, but he'd trained. Hard. Had enough encounters under his belt he hadn't been worried he wouldn't measure up. Would miss his target or freeze under pressure. But all this water shit?

There was a reason he'd always stuck to the air. Why he hadn't ventured outside his vocation like Xavier. Booker was a pilot, through and through. Had been born with hollow bones, according to his mother. One of the only memories he had of her. So, knowing Calliope was counting on him not to let them both drown…

He'd man up. Push past his limits, but he definitely owed the rest of his crew a healthy dose of respect because if this was the kind of shit they'd done day after day, he'd greatly underestimated their prowess.

The fact Callie was still conscious — kicking and trying to swim with her other arm — definitely helped the situation. Got them within reach of the bank quicker than if Booker had been dragging her. Trying to swim against the current on his own. Actually finding sure footing and hauling themselves out took several tries, including one where they slipped and were swept out, again. But with steady persistence and that luck he'd been pushing, they made it onto the shore.

Callie collapsed beside him, her chest heaving, limbs shaking. Whether from the cold or exhaustion Booker wasn't sure, but there was no denying they were both riding the edge. Were close to all those limits he'd been surpassing. He was just about to roll over — see if she was okay or seeing double from the obvious head injury — when she bolted upright. Gave his arm a firm tug.

He levered onto one hand, scouring the area. "God, please don't tell me there're alligators or something in this river because I really don't want to have to wrestle one, right now."

"No alligators. Though, I think there might be some caimans or something…" She grunted, giving him a shake. "Mercenaries, remember?"

"Hard to forget, but if they chose to follow us down that embankment, they're crazy. And probably dead because I'm fairly certain we just used up all nine lives." He nodded at her head. "You okay? Seeing double? Feel like you're gonna puke?"

"Yes, to all three." She shivered, though he wasn't sure if it was because she was cold or from everything else. "When that damn ledge gave way… I can't believe you followed me. You're crazy. You know that, right?"

He grinned. "Just about you."

She swatted him, again. Harder.

He grabbed her hand, bringing it to his mouth for a soft kiss. "When you disappeared…" Christ, he'd thought he'd lost her.

"Sorry, but you're not getting rid of me that easily. You promised me bacon, remember?"

"You're the one who's frying the bacon, sweet-heart." He shivered as more rain pelted his face. "We need to find somewhere to wait out this damn storm, assuming it doesn't become a full-fledged hurricane. I don't suppose you know where we are?"

Callie pushed to her feet, swaying a bit before offering him her hand — helping him up. "Sure. We're on a riverbank in Puerto Rico. Probably still in El Yunque."

"Your powers of perception are frightening. Okay, we stick to the riverbank and hope we find a trail or two-track that leads to some sort of shelter. Pray this weather keeps Keith and his mercenaries busy. Just, try not to go for another swim."

She leaned in close, dragging one strong, tiny finger across his chest like she'd done a few times, already. "What's wrong, Booker? Swimming not part of that training you took?"

"Let's just say this body was born to fly."

"I'll try to remember that. Stay close. With every-thing whipping around, it would be easy to become separated."

"Are you asking me to keep my hand on your ass? Because that's a sword I can fall on."

"Wyatt's right. You're a jerk."

"Hell, yeah. Okay, we stick close. And once we find someplace to rest, we're having a long chat about why you thought it was a good idea to confront your old boss on your own. And yeah, I know it probably saved our asses but…"

But he wasn't sure he could survive another round of her trying to sacrifice herself for him. And the sooner she understood that, the better.

CHAPTER 8

TALK ABOUT A SHITSTORM...

Callie wasn't sure which part of the mission was the most screwed up because they'd been dodging one catastrophe after another since they'd landed. First the car chase, then the helicopter. She'd thought they'd faced the worst of it until her damn boss had turned out to be the asshole who'd set her up. Even falling down the mudslide and nearly drowning in the river seemed oddly comforting compared to realizing her entire career had been a lie.

Or at least, the people in it.

That's what stung the most. That she'd looked up to him. Considered him a mentor. Hell, a friend. Discovering he'd been playing both sides for god knew how long had her questioning if she still believed in what the DEA stood for. If she'd be able to find her way back once this op was over.

Assuming they didn't die from exposure or get swept away by the damn storm threatening to tip a tree over on top of them at every turn. While she'd survived tropical storms and hurricanes before, she'd never been hiking through the forest during one. And knowing she might be the reason Booker didn't make it…

No, she wouldn't think like that. Booker was tough. More than tough. The man was a machine. Even now, he was leading the way, breaking branches and ensuring nothing surprised them while keeping them moving when she knew they both just wanted to sit down and sleep. Right there in the jungle, the tropical storm raging around them. Every inch of them soaked and shivering.

But after all he'd done — following her down a freaking embankment — she wouldn't be the reason they didn't find someplace to wait out the storm. He'd been right. There was no way Keith or any of his men would be out searching for them, now. Sure, if they hadn't disappeared, she had no doubts the bastards would have trailed behind them until they'd run out of rainforest. But whether she wanted to acknowledge it or not, nearly dying falling down that stupid escarpment had stayed any confrontation until the worst of the storm had passed.

Booker stopped in front of her, and she nearly plowed into him before she caught herself — managed to only knock into his back. He didn't say anything, holding up one first before crouching behind some trees. Waiting for her to copy him then waving at something off to their right.

Callie scanned the forest, squinting in an effort to see anything amidst the rain and leaves, only to inhale when she saw the wall hidden within the brush not far off. What she assumed was another shack the cartel used to store drugs or weapons. One of the ways they avoided capture if local law got too close.

Booker glanced at her, making more hand signals. He'd go left while she went right. She nodded, slinking around to one side as Booker disappeared in the opposite direction. She moved slowly, checking every direction before taking another step. Wishing she hadn't lost her damn weapon in the river.

Booker had offered her his Sig, but she'd refused. Between the double vision and the pounding in her head, she wasn't ashamed to admit he was probably the better shot, right now. Might be the better shot, regardless. And with the amount of kickback his Sig had, he had more of a chance of eliminating a target than she did when her arms felt so heavy, she wasn't even sure she'd be able to lift the damn thing, let alone keep it steady. He hadn't argued, giving her a knife instead. One she assumed he'd kept in an ankle holster. Or maybe he'd had it on his belt. Regardless, it gave her a slight advantage if they met with any resistance that wasn't armed.

She nearly laughed at the thought. Since when were mercenaries or cartel members not armed? Never, in her experience. But she allowed herself a bit of false hope. Tried not to dwell on the fact she was the weak link in their current partnership.

Booker waved at her once she'd circled the perimeter, waiting at the door before shoving it open, then motioning her inside. "I was able to see enough through the cracks in the boarded window to be confident it's empty."

She nodded, still checking every inch of the small space before settling down beside him on an old crate pressed up against the wall. Just like the ones they'd hidden behind back in the shack where everything had gone for shit. Again.

Booker wrapped his arm around her, tugging her in close. "While I know we need to get out of these wet clothes, I just can't seem to muster the strength to care, right now."

She snorted. "You and me, both."

"You okay? Still seeing double?"

"More just blurry shifting, now, but yeah, I'm fine."

"You're more than fine, but that's not what I asked." He lifted his arm, gently twisting her chin until she was looking at him. He held up two fingers. "Well? How many?"

"Two."

He frowned. "One."

She inhaled, squinting a bit more before giving him a shove. "No way. There's definitely two."

"But the fact you questioned my reply means you guessed." He tilted her head. "That cut really should have stitches, or at least some skin adhesive, but the med kit is trashed."

"Aw, don't worry, Booker. It just means I'll have a matching set of scars, now."

"Not funny." He muttered something under his breath, still turning her head to each side. "The only good thing about that trip down the river is that it kept the swelling down — stopped the bleeding."

"Yeah, slipping down that mudslide was a real lucky break."

"You're alive. I'd say that's as lucky as we can get." He leaned forward, getting dangerously close. "Do *not* scare me like that, again. And here I thought you confronting Keith was as bad as it was going to get."

"We didn't have many options, and I knew the bastard wouldn't outright shoot me."

"You *hoped* he wouldn't."

"It worked, didn't it? You were scary awesome, by the way. Throwing that smoke grenade. I swear Keith shit his pants thinking it was a flash bang."

Booker simply shrugged. "I didn't have many options with that guy standing in the shadows with his gun at the ready."

"Too bad Keith dove for cover, or we could have taken the bastard out of the equation for good.

Because we both know it won't be truly over until he's either dead or in custody."

Booker stopped scanning her head for more injuries and stared at her. Eyes narrowed. Mouth pinched tight. "I couldn't risk that the asshole at the door wouldn't kill you if I tried to cap Rogers, first. If I'd thought I could have hit them both…"

"Mission isn't over, so you might still get your chance."

"Just like we got to swim."

"I aim to please. Sorry I didn't have a bikini handy."

God, the way Booker smiled. All sexy lips and dark stormy eyes. It made the rest of the shack tilt, and not because of how hard she'd hit her head.

He got impossibly closer, his warm breath mixing with hers. "Trust me, that shirt leaves very little to the imagination. Speaking of which… we really should strip out of the big stuff before exposure sets in."

"And how will being basically naked stop us from freezing our asses off?"

"I've got one of those survival blankets in my pack. They don't really stay wet, and we can share it and body heat."

Christ, he was serious. He wanted them to strip down and huddle together wearing only the essentials. Not that she didn't want to feel every strong inch of his skin against hers. She just wasn't sure she'd be able to keep things professional. That, the moment he took her in his arms to share body heat along with the blanket, she wouldn't jump him.

Booker chuckled, the bastard, as if he'd followed her train of thought. Knew exactly how close to the edge she was where he was concerned. Knowing she owed him her life didn't help stem the instant punch of lust when he stood, offering her his hand.

She swallowed, damn near choked when he smiled, again, then placed her palm in his. Smacking into his chest when he yanked a bit too enthusiastically only increased the jumpy feeling in her gut — made it harder to breathe the closer he moved.

Booker leaned down, not quite touching her. "Easy, sweetheart. I promise to be a complete gentleman... If you want me to."

God, his voice. The hint of southern drawl in it. How it sounded deeper than usual. Lower. Like well-aged whiskey on ice. Hot and cold all at the same time. It sent goosebumps racing across her skin. Had her primed with nothing more than the suggestion of more.

The concussion. Surely that was why she'd lost her mind. Why she wanted to tiptoe up — taste that cocky mouth when they were hiding in the middle of the jungle in a damn cartel drug shack.

Booker laughed, the deep, raspy sound igniting all her nerve endings, just like the lightning had when it had struck the chopper. "You really must have hit your head if you're this tied-in-knots at the thought of me seeing you naked." He dipped down. "I *have* seen you naked before, you know."

She smiled, brushing her mouth across his without actually kissing him. "It's not you seeing me that's got me tied-in-knots."

Had he inhaled because of what she'd said or because he was having a hard time breathing, too? Like in the Jeep when she'd sworn the broken window was sucking out all the available oxygen.

He stayed close, inhaling deeply as if scenting her, before reaching for his jacket. "I'll leave on the sexy boxers, if that makes it easier for you to... concentrate."

Right, like seeing his ass and groin stretching the tight cotton fabric was going to ease anything. In fact, she had a feeling it would only make her want to strip that last bit of clothing off, even more.

Booker took her silence as permission to continue, quickly shucking his clothes then hanging them on one of the other crates. Not that they'd fully dry, but it was better than leaving them in a heap on the ground. Then, he turned and started scrounging through his pack. Removing a bunch of items along with that ridiculously thin survival blanket.

He sighed, laying some of the pictures on the floor. "These photos are ruined. Most likely the recorder, too, though, Wyatt and his brainy IT mind might recover something. But at least the camera

Charlie got you was waterproof. I swear the guy thinks of every scenario. Creepy, really."

Callie stripped down to her bra and panties, shivering when the wind whipped through the holes in the boarded-over window. "I just hope it's enough because we really could have used those photos and the crappy splicing job to seal the fucker's fate."

He glanced over his shoulder, pausing to give her a thorough once-over, before winking. "It definitely would have helped... Luckily for you, I recorded the entire exchange on my phone."

"You what?" She closed the distance, crowding him when he simply stood there, smirking. "Booker, I'm serious!"

"So am I." He grabbed the phone he'd placed on the crate beside his clothes. "Assuming the damn thing still works after all that time in the river..."

Callie held her breath as he activated the app, then played the recording. The voices were tinny, slightly muffled, and the battery died before they got all the way through, but it was enough to soothe her doubts. Though, just hearing how breathy she'd sounded...

Not quite scared but definitely upset. And she had been. Discovering Keith had actually ordered mercenaries to kill her...

Booker sighed, then hugged her against him, pressing her head into the crook of his shoulder while he palmed the small of her back. Protecting her against whatever he'd been worried was bouncing around in her head. Maybe another PTSD moment, like she'd had in the chopper. Not that she'd realized he'd noticed. Though, looking back, it had been foolish to think he hadn't.

"Breathe, sweetheart. It's all going to be okay."

She wrapped her arms around his back, allowing him to shoulder some of the strain. Even if it was only for a moment. "I thought that's what people said when things got desperate."

"We're in a shack in the middle of the rainforest, with a squad of armed drug cartel hunting us down, and a tropical storm raging around us. I'm sure that level of desperation will eventually crop up."

She laughed. God, she was crazy about the guy. Not just because he looked like sin. It was how he knew exactly what to say to ease the tension. Make her believe they really would come out of this mess in one piece. How he'd been willing to die in order to save her. He hadn't said it, but she hadn't missed the way he'd blocked her from any possible hits while racing through the jungle. Then, he'd followed her down a damn mudslide without knowing if the ride would kill him before dragging her ass out of the river.

The guy was incredible, and she wasn't sure she'd be able to hold back telling him how she felt much longer. That she'd been falling for him long before they'd finally gotten a taste of what it could be like between them that one night. How she'd been in limbo this past year, waiting. Hoping they might get one more chance.

That she was pretty sure this was that once-in-a-lifetime love she'd heard about.

Booker gave her a squeeze. "Let's get comfy. Warm up. Then, we can take stock. Spend some time finding our location on the map. Thankfully, it's waterproof, too."

"Does it have a built-in *you-are-here* feature? Because I'm not sure I even know what direction north is."

"That way." He thumbed toward the door, the ass. As if he actually knew.

"Booker..."

"Pilot. Trust me. I'll find our location on the map."

"Okay, *Indie*. Give it your best shot."

"Brat. Warmth, first. Then the map. And no funny business. You promised you'd cook me bacon after I had my way with you, and I don't compromise when there's bacon at stake."

CHAPTER 9

BOOKER LEANED against the wall as Callie drifted in and out of sleep in his arms, her body snugged into his. All that smooth skin pressed against him. She'd passed out minutes after joining him on the crate, the obvious adrenaline dump sucking out the last of her strength. Unlike him.

He was wired. Borderline twitchy. But not because of the firefight or the subsequent chase. Even the trip down the embankment and along the river wasn't behind his increased breath or how his pulse tapped wildly beneath his skin.

It was her. Calliope Jensen. Special Agent, and the woman he wasn't sure he could live without.

Not that this realization was an epiphany. He'd suspected all along she was the reason he hadn't moved on. Hadn't started dating once he'd been healed enough to think about the future. She'd stolen his heart that night in Virginia, and he hadn't been ready to ask for it back. Reclaim it.

Spending the past two days with her had made him acutely aware that he didn't want it back.

Callie mumbled something in her sleep, her lips pursing into a frown. He gave her a light squeeze, and dropped a kiss on her head, smiling when she settled. As if he was enough to keep the nightmares at bay.

Christ, what she did to him, and she didn't even have to be awake to affect him. Grab him by the balls. Or worse, his heart.

Booker sighed, knowing it was futile to pretend he hadn't fallen in love with her long before they'd both gotten waylaid a year ago and had their lives irrevocably changed. Something the mission had brought to the forefront. Not that he wanted to deny it, it was just... as Callie would say... complicated.

He wondered if she felt at all the same. If she thought they were worth a real shot. Sure, she'd said she'd wanted to call him back. And there was the part where she'd told him she'd wanted more during that fateful night. Had made it clear she wanted them to finish what they'd started. But with everything else in her life circling the drain, he couldn't help but worry their *second chance* might become collateral damage.

"Call me crazy, Booker, but you look like Wyatt just broke up with you."

He snapped his focus down, shaking his head at

that blue gaze. How her eyes gleamed in the dim light streaming in through the cracks. What he assumed was the sun rising, though, it was nothing more than a hint of lighter gray amidst the storm.

"Wyatt would never break up with me. I'm a keeper."

"Not going to argue with that. Then, what's with the look?"

God, if she only knew...

"I was thinking."

"About how screwed we are? Can't argue with that, either."

"We're not screwed. We're just—"

"Out of options? Our minds?" Her mouth quirked into the beginnings of a smile. "Time, maybe?"

"I was going to say, in limbo. Until we figure out our next move. Then, we'll kick ass, again."

Those kissable lips of hers pursed as her eyes narrowed. Then, she was twisting in his arms — rubbing her crotch against his, and damn if his dick didn't respond. From controlled to a full-on boner in two seconds flat. And with them both barely dressed, there was no way she didn't feel him nudging her cleft.

Realizing he wasn't the only one aroused didn't help him regain any of that control. Rein it all in when it was obvious she was right there with him. Waiting.

Booker closed his eyes, inhaling in hopes of

calming the pounding of his heart, but it only infused her sweet scent into his brain. Roses with a hint of summer rain. He didn't know if it was some kind of long-lasting perfume or just her, but he knew he'd recognize it anywhere.

Callie closed the mere inch between them, drawing her finger along his jaw. "I don't want to be in limbo, anymore. Not after spending the past year treading water. Hoping I'd get another chance to have you in this very position. I know the timing sucks. And yeah, there're armed assholes hunting us down, but..."

She nipped at his lower lip, grinning when the moan he'd been suppressing surfaced. "If they were going to chance the storm to come after us, they would have knocked down the door, already. And since it's still raging out there, and the roof and walls seem to be holding..."

She kissed him. No brushing her lips across his jaw, lingering in the anticipation. Just her mouth crushing against his, her tongue tracing the seam until he opened - tangled his with hers. And damn if it wasn't better than he remembered. The warm press of her skin. The velvety feel of her mouth.

Booker didn't push to seize control, knowing she probably needed to expend some of the pent-up energy. The tension and adrenaline from the mission — discovering her boss had been the bastard hiding

in the shadows, all along. But once she eased back...
grabbed a quick breath.

He was all in. Spearing his fingers through her
hair, tilting her head back, then diving in. Making
her kiss look chaste. Like they might have done
during a chance meeting with friends. Not the no-
holds-barred assault he'd launched. Eating at her
mouth, lifting, nipping, then claiming her, again.
Over and over until he wasn't sure either of them
were actually breathing. More likely hoping their
lungs would fill through osmosis. Some weird skin
absorption.

Callie moaned, the raspy sound scratching at all
of his nerve endings already strung tight. Threatening to snap from one more gasp. The lightest of
touches. Having her pull back, then stand, fighting to
remove the last two scraps of clothing had him
following her up. Shucking his boxers before stopping cold because...

God, she was stunning. With sun-kissed skin atop
an athletic frame. Curves that fit perfectly against
him. Complemented his harder angles.

She took a step forward, the gray light hitting her
left side — making her new scars stand out. He
frowned, drawing his fingers along her ribs, circling
the puckered marks before looking up at her.

Callie wrapped her fingers around his wrist,
shaking her head. "Ancient history."

"I should have capped the fucker back at that shack."

"But that's what sets you apart. Makes you the guy who can never be bought. Who I'll always be able to trust with my life." She moved closer, tracing his scars. "You've got some new ones, too."

"Those are all on me, no one else."

"I read the report, Booker. You were the only reason your entire crew wasn't killed. But... I know that's not how you see it. That nothing I say will ease the guilt. Something else we have in common. So..."

She ran that hand across his stomach then down to his hip, stopping with her nails teasing his groin. "How about we forget about the scars. Our failures. And focus on how hot this is going to be. You did say it would exceed expectations."

"So, no pressure."

She laughed. "No pressure, because you've already blown any other lover out of the water just standing there naked."

Christ, she was serious. The easy tilt of her lips, how her smile crinkled her eyes. She meant every word and he hadn't done more than kiss her.

Callie reached down — ran her closed hand up and down his length. "Now, are you going to keep overthinking this, or are you going to finally make love to me?"

"Like there's any other answer than hell, yeah. Just, are you sure you're okay? Not seeing double?

Feel like you're gonna puke from that lump on your head?"

"I'm going to die from sheer sexual frustration if you keep stalling. Does that count?"

"Humor me." He held up two fingers, again. "How many?"

She grinned then squeezed his dick, this time. "I'd say several inches."

He was definitely a goner.

He smiled, grabbed her hand, easing it free before pressing against her. "Dangerous, sweetheart. Especially, when I don't plan on taking any prisoners."

"Good, because I'm not going to surrender easily, either."

Well, damn...

That's all he needed. A scoop and a lift, and he had her in his arms — was twisting them around. A couple steps, and they were back at that crappy crate. The only thing in the shack that saved them from the even worse floor. But... he wasn't about to stop because they didn't have candles and some silk sheets.

A pillow would have been nice, but he'd improvise. Use his pack if necessary. Maybe some of the clothes. Even still wet, they'd beat the grimy floor.

Callie didn't seem to have any concerns about the crate, the floor — hell the shack. Didn't even register when her back hit the wall, her ass riding the wooden box. She just dragged him down to her, claiming his mouth until he really was seeing dots. Not that he cared. He'd willingly pass out before he asked her to ease up — let him breathe.

Having her kiss her way down his neck, biting at the corded muscles, allowed him to gasp in some air. Shake off the dizzy feeling. He wasn't sure if it was from the lack of oxygen or her drugging kisses, but he took a few deep breaths. Was already planning his next move when she made her way back to his mouth. Kissed him, again.

Paradise. That's what this was. Not being on an island in the rainforest, even if the weather had been perfect. No armed assholes gunning for them. It was Callie. *She* was his paradise.

Callie paused when he tsked at her as she tried to go to her knees, raising a brow in question. But he had other plans, starting with her ass still planted on that crate, her thighs draped over his shoulders.

She didn't resist when he slid her back into place. Her gaze locked on his as he kneeled on the floor, running his fingers along the underside of her legs. Teasing the soft spot behind her knees.

That had her giggling, and damn, it spiked his need. Had him vowing he'd do everything in his power to hear that sound, again. Keep that smile curving her fucking gorgeous lips.

He dropped a kiss on the inside of one thigh, then bent her leg over his shoulder, repeating everything on the other side until she was braced against the wall, thighs wide, completely open for him.

She inhaled, as if she hadn't thought he'd have her in this position. That he'd go straight to pinning her to the wall or maybe chancing the floor.

Booker shushed her, running his fingertips along her skin, loving how her muscles twitched in response. "God, you're beautiful."

She sucked on her lower lip, closing her eyes for a moment when he trailed his finger along her wet flesh, swirling it around the tiny nub. "Desperate. That's what I am."

Her head fell back against the wall when he dipped forward — licked her. "Damn, Booker."

He made another pass, humming against her skin. "I love how you say my name. Maybe when we're out of this mess, I can make you scream it."

"You don't have to… yes…"

That word. It spurred him on. Had him licking and nipping, teasing her with barely there touches. Taking her within a breath of her release only to ease back — allow her to come down. She'd started chanting a version of his name a while ago. What he assumed was her way of telling him she needed more. That he was running out of time.

He'd kept going, wanting her to be so blinded with need, she threatened to kick his ass. That "better than mind-blowing" pinnacle he'd promised to take her to.

He wasn't sure how long he'd had her beneath him, perched on the edge, before she yanked on his hair — met his gaze.

"Booker, for the love of god, either send me over or thrust inside. Because if you keep me hanging here, one more second..."

She'd do some crazy DEA ninja move. Maybe shoot him in the ass with his Sig. That's what the furrowed brows and piercing stare suggested.

Booker leaned forward, wedging her thighs farther apart as he brushed his mouth over hers. Drank in her next gasping breath. "Now, we've reached the right level of desperate. Hold on, sweetheart, this ride's about to get bumpy."

CHAPTER 10

Now, she was desperate enough? When she'd been practically begging him for the past thirty minutes. Or had it been an hour? She wasn't sure. Didn't have the strength to check because...

He'd been relentless. Drowning in her arousal as he'd continuously taken her to the edge without ever pushing her over. Giving her just enough time to ground herself before repeating everything. Taking her to the brink, again.

Callie couldn't wait, any longer. Not when her voice was already hoarse from saying his name. Her fingers cramped from clenching his hair. And if he kept her thighs wrapped around his massive shoulders for one more minute, she wasn't sure she'd be able to move them.

Booker seemed completely oblivious to how far gone she was. That, or he was enjoying it, the sexy bastard. And she swore she'd get her revenge. Tease him for twice as long after she'd recovered from this session. Once he'd finally eased the fire burning beneath her skin.

Having him pick her up was unexpected. Had her gasping in a quick breath before he was twisting — laying down on the floor with her straddled over him. Which only confirmed her suspicions that the guy was nuts. If he thought she had the energy to actually ride him...

He smoothed his hands up her thighs, drawing lazy circles across her skin, looking so damn gorgeous she had to fight back tears. He was so much more than she'd bargained for, and she knew she'd never be able to go back to how it had been before this mission. Nothing but work. Forever living a lie. She wanted more.

She wanted him.

Booker paused, hands cupping her hips, gaze centered on her before he sighed, pushing up until she was trapped between his thighs and his chest. "Do I want to know what you're thinking? Because you seem a hundred miles away, which doesn't speak much to my ability to go beyond mind-blowing."

She snorted, leaning into him. Loving the way his breath mixed with hers. "You've already gone beyond mind-blowing. And I was just thinking that you're crazy if you think I have any strength left to do all the work."

He studied her, and she knew he was somehow reading beyond the obvious. That he suspected she was hiding something. "I'll help. I just didn't want your back on the floor."

"Baby, I'll take my back on the floor, against the wall, or balanced on that stupid crate and not feel anything but what you're doing to me. You can pick slivers out of my skin for the next week. But beyond that... I just really need you above me. Holding me. Nothing but your gaze locked with mine."

Frozen. That's what he looked like. As if time had stopped, and she was the only one still moving. Hurtling forward. She was just about to snap her fingers in front of his face — see if he really was frozen — when he closed his eyes and rested his forehead against hers.

This had to be love. The two of them in that crappy shack, oblivious to the wind rattling the walls, blowing rain and bits of leaves through the cracks in the boarded window. Nothing really registering but the beating of their hearts. How their chests pressed against each other in perfect sync.

That frozen time she'd just been thinking about.

Booker didn't move, didn't speak, just held her, each exhalation sounding forced. As if he was pushing the air around some kind of lump in his throat. Much like her, only she knew exactly what the lump was. Those three words trying to claw their way free.

Had she actually said them out loud? Groaned? Whispered his name? Because he went from holding her tight, to spinning on his ass, grabbing his shirt, then placing her on top of it. It was still damp, the fabric cold against her back, but she didn't care because he was exactly how she wanted him. His weight braced on his elbows. Every inch of their bodies touching as he stared down at her, his hair teasing his eyes. That perfect mouth lifted into a smile.

She traced her finger along his jaw, grinning at the firm brush of stubble. "Is this going to hurt your elbows?"

"What elbows?"

Definitely love.

He leaned down, kissing her softly, as if she might fly apart if he used more force. "Before we finally do this right, you need to know that I don't have any condoms."

She lifted her head enough to nip at his bottom lip. "Unless this is your way of telling me you have something you shouldn't be sharing…"

"Of course, not."

"Then, carry on, soldier. I'm on birth control, so…"

A strangled groan sounded around them, his head falling to her forehead, again. "Christ. You really are determined to kill me."

"Thinking, if we're gonna die…"

"Agreed. But not today."

He moved, shifting his hips forward, sinking just a hint of himself inside her. And damn if just that small motion didn't set her off. Had her already fighting not to finish because it wasn't just the sex. It was him. Booker Hayes. The man who'd saved her life a dozen times today. And he was finally hers.

She must have moaned, or said his name, because he muttered something under his breath, then thrust forward, filling her with one smooth tilt of his hips. He paused, staring down at her as if waiting for some magical sign she wanted him to move, again, before dipping down — kissing her.

She must have given him whatever he wanted in that kiss because it set him off. Had him sliding out then pushing back in. Harder than before. Deeper. He didn't stop this time, just kept moving. Eating at her mouth as he thrust in, then out.

Heat burned through her veins, igniting the nerve endings he'd just tortured until she wasn't sure how she didn't set them both on fire. Some kind of sexual combustion that would probably take the shack with it. Maybe even the jungle, despite the pouring rain. The possible flooding.

Callie cinched her arms around Booker's back, pulling him closer. Needing more of his weight holding her down. That fear that she really would fly apart if he let go. He must have read her mind because he practically flattened her on that flimsy shirt, making it hard to suck in her next breath.

What she could only describe as heaven.

Another few minutes, and she was gasping to breathe. Not from his weight, but the sheer heat billowing through her core. Like a fire sucking up all the available oxygen. Another five, and she was chanting his name, again. Not loud, her voice already hoarse from his endless teasing, but he definitely heard it. Those two syllables rasped over and over.

Or maybe she was only getting the first out. Regardless, it had him upping his pace. His hips pumping so fast it shimmied them across the floor a bit. Had that shirt bunching up beneath her.

Booker clenched his jaw against her neck, grunting through the next few strokes before latching onto her shoulder. Giving her a firm love bite.

She broke.

No further build-up. No swirling of that heat in her belly then shattering outwards. She simply imploded. Whole one moment, then a thousand tiny pieces the next. Like the window in the Jeep. Nothing but fragments reflecting the dim light.

Booker kept moving, sending her higher before he rasped her name and emptied inside her in a series of jerking thrusts. What seemed to go on forever before he collapsed on top of her. Muscles still tense. His forehead resting on hers.

Definitely heaven.

Booker sucked in a few breaths, then tried to push to his elbows. It took him a few attempts, but he managed, finally staring down at her with those gorgeous eyes all bright and shining. Those shadows she'd noticed from earlier gone. Shattered like she'd been.

He smiled, and her stomach fluttered. The good kind with all the butterflies skittering around. The heat from earlier rekindling into a slow, warm burn. "Damn, sweetheart. I recognize that look. Are you jonesing for round two, already?"

She grinned, then punched her hips up a bit. Reminding him he hadn't slipped out, yet. "I doubt I'll ever not be ready where you're concerned. That..."

"I'll assume it met expectations?"

"Baby, you had any expectations exceeded before we even started. Simply getting naked did that. Making love to me..." She blew out a rough breath. "Let's just say it'll be worth you pulling slivers out of my ass for the next week."

He frowned, as if taking stock of where they'd ended up, then closed his eyes. Groaned. "You should have told me I was shoving you across the damn floor."

"You say that like I even noticed. Or cared. Already told you, you're worth it."

"Let's hope you still feel that way when I have to

poke you in the ass."

Callie pushed onto her elbows, closing the distance between them. "Love me like that, again, and you can do anything you want to my ass."

Was he breathing harder? Quicker? Or was that her chest pressing rapidly against his. Her heart bouncing around in her ribs.

"Didn't the DEA teach you not to write blank checks?"

"They did. I just chose to break that rule where you're concerned. After all, you did say you'd always have my back. Be the one man I know I can trust."

"Remind me not to say things in the future that will curtail what filthy things I can do to you." He eased over, grunting when he slipped free. "I swear I'd trade just about anything, right now, for a bed."

She rolled onto her side. "I think we did just fine without one."

"Hell yeah. But just thinking you might get scraped or cut…" He sighed, and damn if his statement didn't pool tears behind her eyes. No one had ever worried about her like he did.

She smiled, running her finger along his chest. "I'm a big girl. I don't mind a bit of rough play. But it sounds like you're tabling those naughty things until we have better surroundings."

"That, and because we need to figure out where we are and be ready to leave as soon as the storm dies down a bit. Bad guys with guns, remember?"

. . .

"HARD TO FORGET. Fine, we'll put round two on rain check status. But know this…" She leaned in close. "The next adventure will start with me on my knees until you beg me for mercy."

Booker swallowed. Hard, coughing a few times as if it had been difficult, before dropping a kiss on her lips. "Consider it a date."

She sighed when he stood, offering his hand before helping her up. He ran his fingers down her spine to her ass, then grunted and grabbed a sock. A quick breath, as if he was preparing himself for something unpleasant, then he was darting outside, dancing in the rain for a second before rushing back in and using it to clean both of them.

She inhaled at the brush of cold, damp fabric across her skin. "I doubt you needed to stick it in the rain when it was probably still soaked from that ride down the river."

Booker chuckled. "I don't know, sweetheart. You're nearly as wet as the sock."

She grinned, reaching out and wrapping her fingers around his length. "Unless you want those mercenaries to walk in here with me on my knees, you might not want to remind me how desperate I still am."

Booker nodded, though she could tell it was forced. That he wanted her to suck him off — to start round two, right now — as much as she did. But he was right. Though the wind was still howling outside, it sounded as if the rain had eased. And they needed to use what was left of the storm to figure out their next move, or there wouldn't be any more rounds.

She removed her hand. It took three tries and a silent pep talk, but she managed it. Only hissed a few times dragging on the damp clothes. Not soaking like they'd been several hours earlier, but nowhere near dry. Like her. Perpetually aroused because the one man who set her off was only a breath away, looking smoking hot in his clothes. The way they hugged every muscular inch, the wet fabric leaving nothing to her imagination. Not that she needed it because she knew exactly how he felt against her. Inside her.

Booker managed to zip everything inside his skin-tight pants, then scrounged around until he found the map, flattening it out across the crate — the same one he'd practically devoured her on — then looked across his shoulder at her. "Hey. You okay?"

She gave herself a mental shake, trying to focus on what he'd said. "What?"

He smiled. "I asked if you were okay."

"Sure. Why?"

"The look on your face…"

"Can't help it that I'm finding it hard to shift gears."

"Right there with you. So, think of it this way. The

quicker we get out of here, the quicker I can lick every inch of you, again."

Christ, the man was going to kill her with her own desire. "I get first dibs on licking. But you have a point." She ambled over to the crate, gazing down at the map. "You really think you can figure out where we are?"

"Close enough. Where do you think we are?"

She snorted, drawing her finger around the entire El Yunque rainforest. "Somewhere in here."

He chuckled. "You're not wrong." He pointed to a spot inside the rainforest. "This is where we parked the chopper, and this is where the shack was. When we had to escape, we headed north for a bit, then east."

He moved his finger along the map as if he'd memorized their route the previous night. The one where she'd been running blindly through the jungle, praying to stay ahead of the assholes chasing them without dying or falling off a cliff.

He tilted his head, leaning closer to the map before nodding. "You slid down that embankment then into a river most likely around here..." Another trace of his finger across that map then he was grinning. Tapping the damn thing. "Considering we were swept along the river for a good fifteen to twenty minutes, and that the river went around a few bends — took us back toward the west side of the forest..."

Booker drew a circle on the map. "We should be somewhere inside this area, give or take."

Callie stood there, staring at him, wondering if he'd lost his mind. "No freaking way you just sussed that out." She started to pat down his clothes. "You used your phone, right? Some tracking app…"

Booker laughed, snagging her hands before shoving them behind her back as he pulled her against him. He gazed at her mouth, dipping in for one of his drugging kisses before easing back. Keeping her close. "There's no signal up here. Pretty sure none of those texts we sent ever reached our contacts, and my phone died while replaying the message, remember? So, no. I didn't use an app. Just common sense."

"And a GPS shoved up your ass."

"It was a requirement for being part of Flight Concepts."

"I bet. So, assuming you're right—"

"I'm right."

"At least you're not smug about it."

"It's part of my charm."

"Okay, *Columbus*, what's our best way home?"

He pursed his mouth, squinting a bit before shrugging. "Honestly, no idea."

"I thought you were some ace navigator?"

"I said I could find out where we were. I have no idea where any trails are or if the roads around here are flooded. My best guess is we backtrack a bit. See if that shit track we came up on is still walkable. If not, then, we might have no other choice than to hike back to the chopper. With it being higher and on an old dirt road, we should be able to reach it. Because there're a few large ass rivers in every other direction and with how much rain has fallen…"

He met her gaze. "I'm not sure I want to chance the water, again. The current's going to be ten times as strong as it was last night."

"You just don't want to go swimming. I'm on to you."

"Busted. But…"

She silenced him with a lingering kiss. "I agree. I'd rather we take our chances on land, even if we have to hike back up. The only wildcard will be if Keith's discovered the helicopter, yet."

"Do you really think he sent his guys out searching for it in the middle of the typhoon?"

"Probably not. But if the weather's clearing by the time we get up there, I don't see him leaving anything to chance. And there're only so many places you could have landed, though, we did have to hike for hours to reach the shack. Not the likeliest of hiding spots."

She tapped her chin, then shrugged. "Worst case… He found the helicopter, and he'll have men guarding it. Or he'll hide a tracker on it, just in case we sneak past his sentries."

"Bad guys and trackers I can handle. Besides, I've got a secret weapon."

"What's that?"

He kissed her back. "You. And with how pissed off you're gonna be if we have to drag our butts all the way up there, you'll take out his entire force by yourself."

"Ass."

"Hell yeah. We'll pack up. The rain was getting pretty light when I darted outside, so... We should head out. Hope we get lucky, and we can find a useable road that will take use toward the city. But if we can't, we're going to need all the gray daylight we can get just to reach the chopper. And I really don't want to spend another night in this jungle."

"Are you saying last night wasn't pleasurable?"

"I'm saying that I doubt we'll get lucky, twice, and not have any visitors. Besides, I'd really like to have some kind of cushion between us and the floor because... last night was just a taste. Round two is going to blow you away."

"I'll hold you to that." She eased back, grabbing a few items off the floor then stuffing them in the pack. "Booker?"

He arched a brow as he folded the map. "Yeah?"

"Thanks. For everything. I promise, I'll find a way to make it up to you."

"You already did, last night. Though, you still owe me some bacon."

CHAPTER 11

"Well, shit."

Callie sighed as Booker crouched behind a couple of trees, eyes narrowed. His gaze focused on the helicopter parked in the small clearing off to their right. What looked like a dozen armed assholes patrolling the area.

They'd been hiking all day, trying to find a more direct path back to civilization. But between the roads and the weather and what was likely some kind of voodoo curse, they hadn't found a single, useable route. Booker had made the executive decision to retreat back to the chopper before they ran out of time and daylight. And while they'd been able to navigate their way along the old dirt roads without running into a squad of mercenaries, it appeared their luck had finally run out.

Booker huffed, clenching his jaw until the muscle

in his temple jumped from the strain. "This definitely puts a wrench in our plans, especially with the sun already setting."

She studied the men, mentally mapping out their patterns. "How long do you need to get your baby airborne?"

"I made sure she was ready for takeoff before we left. But even with everything in place, I'll need a minute." Booker glanced at her. "And since I can't crank on the engine without making any noise, that's probably fifty-five seconds more than we'll get before they fill us full of holes."

Callie nodded, running through various options in her head. But no matter how she looked at it, there was really only one solution that might give Booker that minute he needed. "So, what you're saying is… You need a distraction. Something for those good old boys to focus on, instead of you."

Had he grunted? Growled? Callie wasn't sure other than some deep, raspy sound had rumbled through his chest a moment before he turned — took her by the shoulders until she was staring up at him. Those gorgeous eyes searching hers.

He shook his head, glancing over his shoulder at the clearing. "The only way I'd ever say yes to that suggestion is if you're standing here, telling me you know how to start our ride. Because there's no way you're being bait. And yeah, that's what you meant, you just made it sound less risky. Like you could simply toss a stone or a stick, and they'd all chase after it like dogs."

"Booker—"

"I realize we don't have many options. In fact, we pretty much don't have any. But I'm not going to sit in that chopper, playing with circuit breakers and rolling on the throttle, while you run off and get yourself shot a dozen times."

"I'm not going to get shot."

Booker scoffed, crossing his arms over his chest. The massive one she'd used as a pillow all night. That she wanted to trace with her fingers and tongue. "I'm sorry. I must have missed where you'd packed your golden lasso and bracelets. Or have you simplified to merely a cape, now?"

Callie frowned, copying his stance. "Seriously? I'm a DEA agent."

"And there are a dozen, heavily armed assholes just waiting to put you, me, and anyone else who pops their head up, six feet under."

"I'm not going to confront them, merely lead them away long enough for you to get our ride fully functional."

"And when they start firing? Because we both know they'll start firing."

"I can run pretty damn fast."

"Those scars on your rib cage suggest you can't outrun a bullet."

She huffed. "So, if you were the one being the

distraction, would it be okay, then? Would *you* be fast enough?"

The guy growled, again, then fisted his hands at his side, brows furrowed. Slashes of red creeping along his cheekbones. "Don't. Don't stand there and suggest this is because I'm a guy and you're not. I've never treated you as anything other than an equal because you are. But neither of us are bulletproof. And no, Calliope, I can't outrun a bullet, either, as a few of my scars can attest to."

He blew out a harsh breath, then raked his fingers through his hair, spiking it up in every direction. "Have you stopped to think that maybe, just maybe, losing you would kill me? That it's the one thing I wouldn't be able to come back from, and trust me, sweetheart, I'm still fighting my way back from that wreckage. Still trying to find my worth when I know I'm the reason those men didn't make it out of that helicopter, alive. That no matter what anyone says, or how many medals they give me for supposed bravery, I'll never wash their blood off my hands. Never get that chance back to be the pilot they needed me to be."

He rolled his shoulders, closing his eyes for a moment before holding up his head. Looking her dead in the eyes. "There's got to be another option."

He was waiting for her to say something. To answer, but all she could do was stand there and stare at him. Her heart thrashing inside her chest. Her pulse echoing in her ears. He'd been serious. Had all but told her that he loved her, and he'd said it as if it had been easy. Like talking about the weather. Or where they were going to go out for dinner.

And all that stuff about the accident...

She'd suspected he was still healing. *Still dealing...* But knowing he was just as deep into the darkness as she was — that he'd been faking it for the past year hoping no one noticed — screwed with her brain. The agent part that wanted to go in, guns blazing, despite the risk. That needed vengeance a bit more than she wanted to admit.

Booker frowned, reached for her, but she was already stepping into his space, palming his face, then kissing him. Not long and hard like she wanted. This wasn't the time and definitely not the place. But she needed him to know she loved him, too.

He was still frowning when she eased back. "What was that for?"

"Because you're you." She took a healthy step back. "And because I love your sorry ass. And I'm counting on you to save mine."

She grabbed their backpack, nodded, then took off, dodging his attempt at grabbing her, as she made a beeline for the other side of the clearing. Keeping tight to the trees as she circled the area, sticking to the deep shadows covering the forest. And with the sun already hidden behind the distant hills, there were plenty of places to hide.

Booker didn't call her name. He couldn't without bringing the entire contingency of mercenaries to his location, and the man wasn't stupid. He just didn't want to admit they needed a break, and since she couldn't fly the helicopter…

He'd be mad. She knew it. But if her plan actually worked, she'd find a way to make it up to him. It might take a while, but since she wasn't sure she'd even have a job to go back to, she'd have the time. She'd make the time.

There, up ahead. Two of Keith's men standing amidst some trees. Each smoking a cigarette as they talked. Not even scanning the surrounding forest. Exactly what she needed to get the rest of their crew to leave the clearing long enough for Booker to reach the helicopter and get it started. Of course, it also meant she'd have to find a way to get out into the open for him to pick her up, but she could only deal with one crazy idea at a time.

She crept forward, careful not to step on any twigs as she closed the distance — got within fifty feet of them. What looked like the kind of tree she could climb without making a lot of noise. Or worse, falling. She checked the men, again, ensuring they were still talking, then grabbed a few bigger rocks and tucked them into the pack. A quick tightening of the straps, and she was ready to go.

It took her a few tries to get her feet to stick to the bark enough to heave herself up. Find any traction to climb higher. What she suspected Booker would have done without any kind of effort. Just a grab and a pull, and he would have been halfway to the top. Smiling down at her.

God, she hoped he'd forgive her. That he'd understand she needed to save him as fiercely as he needed to save her. That the thought of him dying in the process wasn't something she'd come back from, either.

That she was stupid in love with him.

She'd said it. Had put it out there where it was real. Uncensored. Three words she couldn't take back. Okay, five, but... She'd meant it.

A fact she could think about later, after she'd gotten through this without getting shot. Exactly what Booker feared would happen.

A few minutes in, and she'd reached a tall branch — had most of her body hidden behind the leaves. Another minute, and she'd unpacked some supplies and balanced them on her lap. What she hoped would be enough to send the men racing into the forest after nothing but a ghost. That dog joke Booker had made, but didn't seem so far-fetched, now.

Callie stared at the ground, praying this wasn't a one-way ticket, because she really wanted to spend the future with Booker. Whatever that looked like, whatever they could manage.

She drew the Sig, Booker had been using. The one

he'd insisted she take as they'd closed in on the helicopter. What she assumed was his way of making
sure she stayed safe. Then she ran through her plan
one more time, focusing on the men. Not that she
could see much of them, but it was enough she'd get
off a convincing shot. Probably not fatal, but
wounded worked for her. And the sound would have
the rest of the squad charging toward her.

Another deep breath, a slow exhale, then she
fired. Hit the guy on the left in the shoulder,
knocking him forward into his buddy. They teetered
for a bit, the other man trying to bridge his friend's
weight, before they toppled out of sight. The dull
thud echoing through the forest as the report of the
gun slowly faded.

The guy yelled something in Spanish she
couldn't quite make out, but it didn't matter. The
rest of the crew were already shouting and stam-
peding toward her, their footsteps loud in the
suddenly quiet forest.

Callie slipped farther behind the branches,
praying the guy still crouched beside his fallen
comrade wasn't some kind of expert marksman. That
he wouldn't study the bullet wound too closely —
work out a bunch of trajectories in his head. Figure
out the shot had come from up high. What would be
a death sentence for her.

She waited until the men got closer before
chucking one of the rocks up the path. Throwing the

rest once the footsteps had stopped — what she hoped were the men listening for another clue.

Having them actually race past in the direction she'd tossed the stones eased her nerves a bit. A glimmer of hope that she'd make it back to the clearing without getting shot.

It took her several seconds to reposition herself on the tree, then jump down. She rolled once she'd landed, grunting when the items in the pack dug into her back, before she was off and running. Dodging through the undergrowth as fast as possible toward the helicopter. Hearing the engine spool up as she punched into the clearing gave her an extra boost. Had her sprinting toward the machine, until a lone gunman stepped out across from her, semiautomatic rifle aimed at Booker.

She altered her stride enough to get off a couple of shots — catch the mercenary in the chest before he'd opened fire and likely killed Booker in the process. The force knocked the gunman back, but he didn't crumple the way she'd expected. Just stumbled a few steps before straightening. Pointing the muzzle her way.

Kevlar. Or some other kind of body armor. Regardless, there was nothing she could do other than dive onto the muddy ground. Pray the bastard missed. That she'd be able to get off a couple more rounds when he paused to see if she was dead. What might save her life if he didn't kill her, first.

The initial spray kicked up the dirt in front of her, dangerously close to her head. A few precious inches the bastard was sure to correct any second.

Until Booker picked up the helicopter — swept it sideways across the ground. The sheer force of the downwash knocked the mercenary back. The guy regained his balance, but Booker was already turning. Spinning the chopper — using the tail rotor like some kind of weapon.

The engine whined, the changing pitch followed by someone screaming — what sounded like flesh hitting something solid — before the helicopter was gliding across the grass. Knocking over a few of the other men who'd circled back, then blocking anyone else from entering the clearing. He spun the machine around, sent anyone still standing scattering for cover, then slid over toward her, motioning for her to get her ass into the cockpit.

She pushed up, slipped on the mud a couple times, before she was running for the door. More bullets pinged off the fuselage as she jumped in, but they faded into the background as Booker tilted the nose forward — started racing across the ground. Just like back at the airstrip. Nothing but the grass whizzing past as everything blurred into an eerie gray. He banked to the side, then climbed, constantly checking their six until the clearing vanished, the forest spread out in front of them like a smear of death against the horizon.

She leaned against the seat, tossing the pack into the back before glancing over at Booker — trying to judge how pissed off he was. But he barely met her gaze, too busy scanning every direction, then shoving in some circuit breakers as he adjusted the controls.

A few minutes passed before he grunted, giving her a quick once-over. He looked as if he was going to say something, then simply stared out the bubble, again. Gaze fixed. Hands fisted around the controls. Nothing but utter silence filling the cockpit.

She drew herself up, needing to say something to break the oppressive quiet. "Can you just yell? Or rant, or bank the helicopter all over the sky until I puke? Anything but what I can only assume if going to be the silent treatment. After all I've said, I think I deserve more than that."

He pursed his lips, staring at her for less than a second. "You hit?"

She shook her head, even though he was focused on the clouds, again. On what appeared to be more bad weather looming in front of them. "No."

He nodded, clenching his jaw before finally staring at her. All that blue-green gaze demanding her attention. "Good. Because I swear, when this is over, we're going to have a long hard chat about—"

"How reckless I am. Yeah, I know. But it was the only option."

"We could have tried walking out."

She laughed, holding up her hands when he

glared at her. "I know, it's not funny. I just don't see how trying to avoid even more drug cartel would have been safer. Keith and his men aren't the only assholes in that rainforest out for blood. Not to mention, we'd already tried walking out, and couldn't get past the damn rivers. So…"

He didn't comment, just stared straight ahead, hands still fisted around the controls. A permanent scowl on his face.

"You should talk. I thought you always said you couldn't use the blades to chop shit up, like in the movies. That it made it dangerous to fly. Yet, I'm pretty sure you just sliced that guy into a few pieces."

"You shouldn't, and it does. But somehow, letting that asshole blow you away seemed like a worse idea than risking more damage to a helicopter that's already damaged beyond repair."

She sighed, reaching for his hand, thanking every god when he didn't bat her away. "I'm sorry, I frightened you because that's what this is about. You're not mad because I took a risk. You're mad because you didn't have any control over the outcome, and that scared the shit out of you. But before you remind me how insane it was, you should know one thing."

She waited until he made eye contact. "I couldn't live through losing you, either."

She released him then tugged at her shirt, using the motion to stem the shaking in her hands. Not from the gunman or nearly dying. But from thinking that she might have miscalculated how far she could push Booker before he simply walked away. That, in an effort to save him — save her freaking soul — she might have lost him.

Booker huffed, rolling his shoulders the way he'd done a dozen times. The one thing that seemed to ease some of the tension bunching his muscles. Maybe quiet the ghosts in his head. Then, he was shaking his head, smiling at her.

"Damn it, Booker. Say something."

Was he laughing? Because it sounded like that. Loud chuckles that had her swatting him in the chest. Vowing she'd shoot him in the ass as soon as they'd landed.

He glanced over, all sexy eyes with that killer smile. "You are, without a doubt, the most frustrating, infuriating, and incredible woman I've ever known. I was going to tell you that you don't fight fair. That I've never been so proud and so damn scared in my life. That if I wasn't trying to keep this baby upright and going in the right direction — despite the intense vibrations I'm worried might actually shake the entire machine into pieces — I'd kiss you until you begged me to make love to you. And that we're still going to have a very long, likely very loud discussion. But for now, I'll just say, I love you, too, and leave it at that."

Had she died back in that clearing and this was her brain playing out her last wish? Because she was pretty sure Booker had just told her, he loved her.

He laughed, again. "Breathe, sweetheart."

She blinked, still staring at him as she managed to suck in some air. Give herself a shake. "What did you say?"

Booker glanced over, winking, the idiot. "I said, breathe."

"Before that, jackass."

"The part where we're going to have a very long, very loud discussion, including why you just called me jackass?"

"Booker!"

He smiled, and her heart stopped. Just stopped. Beating a thousand miles an hour one second, dead quiet the next. "I said, I love you, too. You were serious back there, right? When you said you loved my sorry ass."

He frowned, looking over at her. "And for the record, my ass isn't sorry. In fact, it's one of my best features."

Callie shook her head, leaning over to his side. "Your ass is incredible. And yeah, I meant it. Every last word."

"Good, because I really didn't want to have to toss you out of the chopper if you'd only been joking."

"Like you'd toss me out."

"Oh, sweetheart. If I had a dollar for every time I've wanted to—"

He inhaled, shoving the helicopter over to one side as muzzle flashes lit up the sky behind them a second before bullets sliced through the chopper. Nearly hitting her in the side as one punched through her door, lodging in the console, instead.

Booker didn't even blink. He just banked the chopper over and started racing for the trees. That big black stain on the bubble taking up her entire view. What she feared would be a very short trip unless he gained some altitude. Fast.

She was just about to cover her eyes when he leveled off. Had that bird skimming along the tree-tops, bobbing in and out of any available hole in the canopy. What felt like the wildest rollercoaster she'd ever been on.

He peeled off when he reached a river, dipping down like he'd done on the flight in. Lodging her stomach somewhere up in her throat when he ducked under a bridge, barely missing both the structure and the water before pitching up. Pushing her back into her seat.

The other chopper whizzed past, banking hard in an attempt to follow them as Booker changed directions. Keeping everything low. Nothing but a few dim stars to brighten the darkness.

He looked over at her, giving her one more killer smile. "Hold on tight. This one's gonna get interesting."

CHAPTER 12

S<small>CREWED</small>.

Just like they'd been when they'd escaped from the landing strip. Only this time, things were far more desperate.

Booker hadn't been completely honest with Callie about the extent of damage they'd sustained during their last flight. That when he'd said they could use the helicopter, again, if needed, he'd meant it as a life or death situation, only. That between the holes in the fuselage and the chips in the blades, it was more than likely they'd only get a few miles out of her before alarms blared through the cockpit, and he lost what few systems were still functioning.

Using the tail rotor to dispose of the mercenary hadn't done Booker any favors. Callie was right. It had been impulsive and reckless. But her life topped everything else. He only hoped the chopper would hold together long enough to get them out of one more crappy situation.

Callie tightened the straps around her shoulders, looking remarkably calm considering the helicopter could quit on them at any moment. Send them headlong into the trees. Assuming he didn't plow it into the water.

Not happening. No way he'd ditch, again. This time, he was going to find a way to win.

He looked behind him, trying to get a bead on the other chopper when more muzzle flashes lit up the sky. Sweeping across his ass end. Narrowly missing any vital systems when he yanked the machine over — had her screaming over the treetops, again.

Not easy with the controls fighting him. All those imperfections in the blades returning to bite him in the ass. He'd just have to man up. Find a way to push through because he wasn't failing Callie.

The thought had him settling in. Using the terrain to his advantage. His machine was small, nimble. Could get in and out of tighter spots than the beast chasing them. What might be their one salvation.

He tipped the nose forward, gaining speed, ignoring the alarm that sounded around them. Sent a loud shrill echoing through the cockpit.

Callie pursed her lips, leaning a bit closer to him. "Booker?"

"I know, sweetheart. Just hang in there. She'll

make it." He sighed when a second alarm burst to life. "Come on, baby, you can make it."

"I really wish you were talking to me, right now. Is there anything I can do to help?"

"Keep an eye on our friend, back there. Let me know if he disappears."

She snorted. "I can't see him until he fires. It's just a big, black mess, otherwise."

"Then, let me know if he's firing at us."

"Pretty sure the bullets flying through the cockpit will give that away, but sure. Anything for you, baby."

Damn, he loved her.

"Booker…"

That's all he needed to change directions, again. Avoid the next round of shots as they went wide, sending ripples along the water. He did his best to zigzag along the surface, the downwash leaving twin waves behind him. The other machine followed, getting level with him as he neared a bend. What he hoped might give them an escape.

He hit the turn going flat out, a low-lying bridge coming up fast. He didn't ease up, everything blurring past them until the last moment. A shift of the controls and they were climbing — barely missing the structure before he banked her over. Hard. Had the machine screaming along some two-bit dirt road. Skids only a few feet off the ground. The rotors just missing the trees. Headlights punched through the darkness ahead of him, and he pulled back, knocking a light off the truck's roof as he soared overtop before sliding back down. Picking up more speed.

Calliope held tight, scanning the area behind them. Shaking her head before looking over at him. "Pretty sure they're still back there. Somewhere."

"No way that machine's fitting inside these trees. They'll be paralleling us. Bastard probably thinks he can catch us."

"And can he?"

Booker snorted. "Not tonight."

"So, the alarms still blaring?"

"Mood music. Get ready, sweetheart. We're running out of real estate, and we aren't slowing down."

If Callie was nervous, she wasn't showing it. No increased breath, or white knuckles. Just that ever-present gleam in her eyes as she nodded, then settled. Her faith in him more than humbling.

All the more reason not to fail. To up his game. Not that it was easy with the controls shaking within his grip, the entire cockpit vibrating from the damage they'd sustained. And without the use of the instruments, he could only guess which systems were close to shutting down. Those alarms he'd brushed off because they didn't have any options. Couldn't land and investigate — wait for backup. Booker was milking the chopper for all she had, aware he'd likely lose the engine or the tail rotor before this was done.

Having the engine chug a few seconds later had

him cursing. Gaining a bit of altitude in case it packed it in. Left him with only a moment to react. He was ready. Had a variety of scenarios mapped out. Not that he had many options with them cruising down the dirt road, forest on both sides, but he'd do his best. Hope it was enough.

Spotting the other chopper overhead, heading for an open section in the trail had Booker rethinking his strategy. Making up another plan, when the radio squawked, a blast of static filling the cockpit.

"If you both want to live, Booker, you'll pull your bird into a hover while we have a chat."

Keith. Though, how the radio was even transmitting was a mystery. Booker had checked it after they'd landed and it hadn't been working.

He yanked back on the controls, fighting the increase in vibrations as the other helicopter swooped in front, filling that open section just as he'd suspected. They faced each other, nothing more than fifty feet and a whole lot of air between them.

Booker keyed up his mike, glancing over at Callie. "Call me crazy, Keith, but I find it hard to believe us living is on your agenda. Not after all the bullets you've put through my machine."

"Those were to get your attention. Encourage you to land. I can't help it if you're too stubborn to know when you're outmatched."

"Is that what you think? That your pilot is better than me?"

"I think our chopper doesn't have a dozen holes in it."

"And yet, we're still breathing."

"Assuming you want to continue breathing, you might want to listen. I have a proposal. All I want is the camera, the recorder and anything else you took. Land, have Callie toss them out, and you're free to go. Though, I suggest you reconsider your next destination. I hear Morocco is lovely this time of year."

A non-extradition country. That didn't bode well.

"You actually think we're going to believe you'll let us go? After all the men you've sent our way?"

"The men were instructed to kill you, not Calliope. Like I said in the facility. She's worth more to me alive, than dead. Though, good help, and all that."

Callie frowned, then punched the dash, activating her mike. "You want to pin this all on me, still, don't you? But it'll look too suspicious if I'm dead, which means headquarters will keep digging. But if I disappear... It proves I'm guilty."

"Higgins really shouldn't have let you come. Now, are you going to be reasonable, or do I shoot you both down and take my chances with whoever steps up to bat, next? Another death that will be on you."

Booker looked over at Callie. Not that he was prepared to surrender, but he needed to know she was with him. That they'd either go down fighting or not at all. She glanced at the rear of the chopper, then around the cockpit, finally settling on the controls. What was her way of telling him she was all in.

He rolled his shoulders, readying his next move when Callie clicked her mike.

"Here's the thing, Keith. You actually have to catch us, to kill us. And I'll bet my life that Booker can outfly your jackass of a pilot, any day. So... screw you."

He was already moving. Tilting the chopper forward — quickly closing the distance between them. What would make it impossible for the other guy to get off a shot before they'd collide. Which had the other pilot reefing on the controls. Tipping her back and up, catching a few branches on the way. What looked like a strike to the tail rotor. Not enough to down it, but it evened the odds a bit. And that's all the advantage Booker needed.

He barreled forward, picking up more speed then cranked her back, making that other guy adjust, again. More reactions that had the asshole heading off to their left. The entire machine shaking as it disappeared into the night.

But Booker was already working through the next five maneuvers. Adjusting the controls when more alarms sprang to life as he kept her climbing, waiting until he'd pushed it as far as possible before pitching her over and screaming toward the ground. Aiming at the other helicopter as it appeared out of the shadows.

Callie inhaled, saying his name as they raced toward the chopper, the wind roaring past the bubble. That incessant beeping louder than before. He didn't backdown, lining up the helicopter when it peeled off, vanishing into the darkness as he banked in the opposite direction. A hint of the city lights brightening the horizon.

Another chug dampened some of his enthusiasm. What might be the last few minutes before the turbine quit for good. Made them an easy target.

He flicked a few switches, deciding on how he'd tell Callie they were probably going down, when she cursed.

"He's back. Heading in from your eight o'clock." She glanced at Booker. "Can a helicopter look pissed? Because this one does."

"Damn, this jackass just doesn't take a hint."

"Shit. We're screwed, aren't we."

She hadn't asked, and he didn't lie. "With any luck, we might reach the landing strip before he catches us, or the engine goes."

"And the bullets he's going to throw at us?"

"Look at it this way… The chopper's already toast. He can't really do much more damage to her."

"Not really comforting."

"I'll get us clear. I prom—"

Another target. Right off their bow and coming in hot. Screaming through the air at some insane speed, nothing but blinking lights as proof it was there.

What guaranteed they wouldn't make it another hundred feet, let alone to the edge of the landing strip.

He'd try to land. Use every last trick up his sleeve just to get one last chance to put her down and let Callie make a run for it. Not his best plan, but he wasn't going to be the reason she died. Not tonight.

He veered off, hoping through some miracle the two choppers collided, when the new machine started firing. Flashes of bright white light amidst the black. Realizing they were aiming at the asshole on his tail was a surprise. One he wasn't prepared for until his radio chirped, static filling the cockpit.

"I swear to god, Booker, if you don't get down here in the next five minutes, I'm going to tell Xavier to shoot your ass down, too."

Un-fucking-believable.

"Wyatt? You sorry son of a bitch, I've never been so damn happy to hear your voice."

"You'd better be happy, jackass, because you ruined my last day with Kirby, so… You freaking owe me big time."

"Anything, buddy, I swear… shit."

Everything went silent. No rattling from the engine or the whine of the transmission, just a chug, a lurch, then silence.

He bottomed the collective, keeping the rpms as high as possible as he scanned the area. But other than the clearing where Wyatt was waiting, there wasn't anywhere suitable to land. His buddy yelled over the radio a second before the thing blew, sending a plume of smoke curling through the cabin.

Callie coughed, though it sounded more like her trying not to puke. "Booker?"

"Everything's going to be okay."

"Which means, we've finally reached that level of desperate you talked about. Anything I need to know?"

"Stay calm, and if we roll, get out as fast as you can and run, even if I'm not with you."

"I'm not leaving you behind...shit."

Her voice cut off as he started flaring the nose up — trading some speed for a bit of height. One last ditch effort to milk it past the final row of trees. Make the edge of the clearing.

Branches clawed as the skids, scratching a line along the fuselage as he tipped her forward, bottoming the collective, again as he crashed through the last bit of foliage before heading for the ground. What looked like a small patch of grass amidst logs and debris. Leftover crap from the storm.

The helicopter shuddered, dropped, then billowed as he raised the collective, one last time, working the pedals to keep the body straight. Hopefully prevent the skids from snagging anything as they bounced onto the grass, catching a bit more air then settling, shaking to a halt another twenty feet ahead.

Not that there was time to celebrate. Two seconds

in, and he was ripping off the buckles, helping Callie out of hers, then grabbing the pack from the back and opening the door. Less than ten, and they were hoofing it across the grass. Putting as much distance between them and the machine. What might be an explosive reaction if the sparks shooting out of the instrument panel ignited the remaining gas. Booker didn't know if Keith's guy had punctured the gas tank, but he wasn't waiting around to find out.

They'd put fifteen feet between them and the helicopter when it blew. No ticking clock or smaller explosion as a warning. Just the sound of their labored breathing then everything going supernova.

Booker managed to shove Callie beneath him — cover her body with his — before debris was flying through the air. One of the rotors embedding into the ground a foot from his head. The sky lit up, the fireball raging thirty feet into the air before easing up. Blanketing the clearing in a thin mist as the rain doused most of the flames, leaving a smoldering mess behind them.

Callie gave him a shove, rolling onto her side as she looked at the wreckage. Mud and grime smeared across her face. Flecks of ash dotting her hair. "Jesus, Booker, your chopper."

He waved it off. "We're still breathing. That's all that matters. Besides, Charlie will get a kick out of putting it on my tab, the bastard."

She frowned, brushing some of the muck off her

clothes. "Is this going to get you in trouble? Jeopardize your new job? I can—"

He kissed her. Swallowed whatever else she was going to say because it didn't matter. His job. The chopper. If he'd end up homeless in order to pay it all off. None of it mattered because she was there. Alive. Her fingers sliding through his hair, her tongue tangling with his as she kissed him back. Practically devoured him on that wet grass, the rain now falling in a steady sheet as more lightning flickered across the sky. The other side of that storm they'd weathered in the shack.

It wasn't until a throat cleared next to him that he managed to pull back. Take stock. Wyatt stood off to his right, arms crossed, frowning. The fact he was already soaked probably didn't help.

He shook his head, offered his hand, then helped her up. "Callie. Nice to see you, again. Glad you're still in one piece." He glanced at the pile of twisted metal, then back to Booker. "At least you didn't have to ditch her in the water."

Booker laughed. "One of life's small mercies. Not that I'm complaining, but how the hell are you standing here, right now?"

Wyatt thumbed toward the hanger in the distance. "Charlie. He called when you missed your check-in. Said something about how I needed to get my ass out of Kirby's bed and down to San Juan. That you were in DEFCON one level shit." Another glance at the wreckage. "Looks like he wasn't exaggerating."

"Great. Now I owe Charlie for sending in the calvary." He looked up when a chopper whizzed overhead. "Shit. I'd forgotten about Keith. We should—"

"Xavier and the crew took care of it. Guess that other pilot isn't quite as savvy as you are. Barely put up a fight once Gunnar and Hunter opened fire — Xavier said something about hitting the tail rotor. Punching some holes in it. That the guy didn't have any other choice but to land. Gunnar's got them hogtied in the back of the chopper, seeing as Xavier managed to keep his in one piece."

"Everyone's a critic."

"It's a gift. Now, are you two ready to get out of the rain, or were you hoping to roast a few marshmallows over the flames?"

"Jackass. And it could have been much worse. Trust me."

"I do, which is why I'm on the ground and not up with the others. You know I won't fly with anyone else unless it's life or death." Wyatt motioned to the truck idling a few feet away. "Jump in. Some DEA bigwig named Higgins already has a quick response team on the way. What's sure to be an epic shit show while they sort everything out. You guys might want to be in some dry clothes before that happens. Then, assuming no one arrests your asses on the spot, we'll try to head home tomorrow."

Wyatt walked toward the truck before glancing back. "Unless you wanted to stay? Do some sightseeing. I hear the rainforest is lovely."

"You really are an ass."

"I know. Now, jump in, before I change my mind and make you walk back to the hanger."

CHAPTER 13

"Calliope? You still with me, sweetheart?"

Callie jumped as Booker's voice sounded in her ear, blinking back the fuzziness. Cringing when she realized she'd passed out in the elevator, leaning against Wyatt in order to stay on her feet. Though, if the guy minded, he wasn't showing it.

She straightened, wiping her mouth to check for drool before tugging on her shirt. Giving Wyatt a curt nod. "Sorry. I guess I blanked out for a moment."

Wyatt merely grinned, watching her stumble out of the unit as if he thought he'd need to catch her. And with how unsteady her legs felt, he just might. "I think I'd be more concerned if you and Booker weren't dead on your feet. It sounds as if it's been a hell of a couple of days."

"Considering we would have just been dead if you

and your team hadn't come along, it could have turned out much worse."

Booker coughed, shaking his head as he palmed his chest. "After all I did to ensure we didn't crash, you're giving Wyatt and the others all the credit for us still breathing? That hurts, Callie."

"Xavier, Hunter, and Gunnar *did* get the other pilot to land. And Wyatt didn't make us walk, so…"

"I'll remember that when you need someone to fly you through a typhoon, again."

She smiled, closing the distance between them, then running her finger along his chest. "Ah, don't worry, baby. You'll always be my hero."

Wyatt snorted. "Baby?"

Booker grinned, and she swore the guy was beaming. "You're just jealous because Kirby calls you jackass."

"Kirby calls every guy jackass."

"Exactly. You're pissed you don't have some cutesy pet name."

"*This* is why she calls you a jackass." Wyatt raked his hand through his hair, nodding at the hallway. "You two steady enough to make it to your room, or do you need an escort?"

"After hiking through the jungle, I think we can manage a carpeted hallway. But thanks for offering."

"See? Jackass." He nodded at Callie. "And you're welcome."

Wyatt took a few steps, then stopped, glancing

back at them. "And Booker *did* finally tell you he's crazy about you, right? The reason you're calling him baby. Why you didn't get separate rooms. Why he's got that ridiculous smile on his face when he hasn't smiled in forever. Because if he hasn't, I'd hate to have to shoot my best friend in the ass."

Booker groaned, shaking his head. "This would be extremely awkward if I hadn't."

Wyatt grinned. "I know."

"You might want to take your own advice, buddy, and tell Kirby that."

"Hey, I can only fix one love life at a time. Get some rest. Our flight's at noon. and I don't want to walk in on anything tomorrow."

Wyatt gave them one last look, reminding them he was only a couple of doors down, then struck off, disappearing into his room.

Booker waited until the guy's door closed before placing his hand on the small of her back — leading her to their door then inside. She managed to stay on her feet all the way to the bed before turning and dropping onto her back.

Had any mattress ever felt this good? Or was it the fact her entire body ached from the past two days?

She bounced a bit as Booker collapsed beside her, his weight drawing her into him. She rolled, resting her head on his chest when he lifted his arm — drew her against him.

If she'd thought it was heaven being with him in a shack in the middle of the rainforest, then this had to be whatever was beyond that. Something higher, with soft sheets and no one actively trying to kill them. Just the sound of his heartbeat strumming against her ear. His fingers making lazy circles along her waist.

She must have hummed, or mumbled his name because he sighed, placing one hand under her chin, then tilting her head up until she was staring into his eyes. That color nearly teal in the streetlight filtering in through the windows.

He smiled, and any thoughts of drifting off to sleep vanished. Gone in two seconds flat. "Come on, sleepyhead. Let's get you stripped down so you can actually get some sleep. Something tells me tomorrow's going to be hell with your boss arriving."

"Higgins is more bark than bite. And I did have permission, remember?"

"To observe. Not have your boyfriend's team shoot your ex-boss' helicopter down, even if the guy's a giant dick."

Boyfriend? Had he actually referred to himself as her boyfriend? And why the hell did that one word set her off. Have her pushing onto her elbows — taking his mouth in hers. Booker inhaled, as if he hadn't thought she'd kiss him. That his words wouldn't have her itching to do so much more than sleep.

He seemed to catch his second wind a minute into the kiss, tugging at her clothes. Yanking pieces over her head then tossing them on the floor. Less than thirty seconds, and she was naked, lying on her back as he shoved his pants over his hips, then kicked them off to one side. A quick shuck of those sexy boxers he'd gone on about and, bam… nothing but firm, hard muscle flexing in the dim light as he prowled across the bed toward her.

She took a moment to drink him in — follow the shadows and dips across his chest and abdomen — before he was straddled above her, his hair teasing his eyes, that sweet mouth of his grinning down at her. "God, you're stunning."

He laughed, easing onto his elbows, as if he'd remembered how much she loved having his weight on her. "By stunning you mean, tough and strong. Killer, really."

She gave him a swat, inhaling when her hand just bounced off of him. "Wyatt's right. You're a jackass. And stunning in every way possible. Which reminds me, I don't think I thanked you for saving my life… again. What you did with that chopper…"

He merely shrugged. "It's not like I made myself bait for a dozen mercenaries."

"No, you just took on them and Keith's crazy pilot in a machine you knew we shouldn't be flying in. How bad was it really damaged?"

"More than you'd like to know. Fine, we'll call a truce for tonight. But come tomorrow…"

She lifted up — nipped his bottom lip. "You'll be coming, again, if I have any say in it, so… give me your best shot, soldier."

He chuckled, then dipped down, taking her mouth with his. Not hard, like she'd thought. This was soft. Coaxing. As if they had nothing but time. Which only did her in, more. Had her running her hands across his back. Digging her fingers into his muscles — trying to drag him closer.

The big jerk resisted for several minutes. Keeping it light. Kissing her with just enough pressure she was practically drowning by the time he deepened his seduction. Moved one hand between her legs. Started rubbing her in quick little circles.

That's all it took. A few passes, and she broke. Hips pumping, nails scratching a line along his side. He kept moving, drawing it out until she was begging him to give her more.

He paused, looking as if he was considering whether to finally starting thrusting or if he was going to wait for her to recover, then keep teasing her.

Torturing her, really. That's what it felt like. Lying there, every nerve on fire as an unrelenting need coiled low in her belly. An ever-present ache between her thighs no amount of foreplay would relieve.

Booker pursed his lips, then smiled as if she'd

reached the right level of desperation, again. Just like back in the shack. Some benchmark only he was aware of.

She resisted smacking him as he shifted his position, settling his hips over hers as she wrapped her legs around him, just in case he reconsidered — decided she hadn't reached critical mass, yet. What might cause her to have some kind of aneurysm or stroke.

Having him bottom out on the first stroke...

It was sensory overload. The leftover adrenaline from the mission, the giddy feeling from having him tell her he loved her, not to mention the sheer pleasure of his body over hers. Nothing but the night between them.

She must have called out his name, or maybe she simply said *more,* because he snapped his gaze down to hers, inhaled, then let loose. No control, no metered strokes, just Booker claiming her with reckless abandon. Exactly what she needed to push her over.

Several strokes in, and she was already cresting. Hanging on that razor's edge, muscles tensed, that coil close to snapping. Another dozen passes, and the bed was tapping the wall — the steady rhythm keeping time with his hips. With every gasping breath she sucked in with the hopes of staying conscious because...

It was too much. The glide of his flesh across hers.

The gravelly way he rasped her name as if just getting those two syllables out cost him. Ate at his control. And when he nipped at the soft spot at the base of her neck...

She imploded. Supernova just like the helicopter, nothing but fire and ash and her soul shattering into a thousand pieces. She latched her mouth on his shoulder, aware she was probably leaving a mark, but unable to stop. To lift off when it was the only way to ground herself.

Booker groaned, then stiffened, emptying inside her in a series of jerking thrusts. Tiny little stabs that drew out her orgasm. Had her drifting into a lulling haze before he'd even finished.

He stayed poised above her for minutes, hours, maybe days later. Anything seemed possible as time simply faded. The sounds outside the window the only indication the world was still spinning.

Callie was still floating when he kissed her eyelids, his gaze finding hers when she managed to blink — stare up at him. And god, he was sexier than ever. Hair tousled. A healthy flush coloring his cheeks that had nothing to do with the weather or having hiked a dozen miles through hostile territory.

He smiled, and her heart thumped. Hard. "You okay?"

She snorted, already drifting, again, when he gave her a slight shake. "Yes, fine, it's just... God, Booker."

Another gut-wrenching smile. "Exactly the kind

of response I was hoping for. Though, if this gets any better, you might just kill me within the first week."

"Like I said. If I've gotta go…" She found enough energy to tilt her head — lose herself in his mouth.

Booker tucked her hair behind her ear after he'd eased back. "I was thinking… It seems a bit pointless to argue about your reckless streak when I know it's part of your genetic makeup."

"It wasn't my DNA flying that helicopter in the middle of a tropical storm, baby. You're just as reckless."

"Fair. So, once we're rested, I'd rather talk about us, and how we're going to make this work. Because I want there to be an *us*, and I want to make it work."

Heat spread along her veins, and she knew she'd found the piece of her she'd been missing. "I want that, too. And who knows, Higgins might can my ass the second we land, so…"

"He'd be an idiot to fire his best agent. And I don't want you to give up what makes you… you."

God, she loved him.

He dipped in for another kiss. "Just promise me we won't be like Wyatt and Kirby. Pretend we're keeping it casual for the next several years."

She brushed her thumb along his jaw. "Pretty sure I already killed that scenario when I told you I loved your sorry ass. And yes, I agree your ass is definitely one of your best features. So, no, Booker, I don't want to keep it casual or play telephone tag. Let's just get this debrief done so I know where I stand with the DEA, okay?"

"Deal. Just know this… I'm not above stealing one of the machines and hunting you down, so…"

"Good to know you're not a stalker."

"Nope. Just the man I hope you're realizing you can't live without."

"I'll keep that in mind. Now… are we cleaning up and going to sleep, or are you up for one more round?" She levered onto her elbows. "I bet I could give you one hell of a blowjob."

His jaw clenched before he was lifting her in his arms — carrying her toward the bathroom. "I hope you don't mind kneeling on the shower floor, because I plan on plastering you to the wall, after. I bet your ass feels like heaven when it cushions every thrust."

"Bring it, flyboy. And you better have saved some stamina because I'm not taking any prisoners, either."

CHAPTER 14

"CALL ME CRAZY, Agent Jensen, but I'm fairly certain your instructions were to *observe* only. Or did I mumble?"

Booker groaned inwardly as Ted Higgins' voice echoed through the conference room, the sharp edge to it impossible to miss. They'd managed to make it back to Montana without any major delays, even if the poor weather had followed them.

Though, why her boss had insisted on going over the evidence, again, tonight when they'd spent all morning justifying every scrap of paper, every damn photo, seemed odd. Though, he suspected it had something to do with the two asshats at his side. More DEA agents who Booker assumed had been sent out to oversee the investigation. Dispel any doubt that it wasn't being given the highest priority.

At least, Higgins had agreed to meet at the new

Brotherhood office. Maintain some separation from the rest of the DEA until the man knew the full extent of how deep Keith Rogers had been entrenched in the cartel's undertakings. If there were more agents involved in the scheme. Which suited Booker, especially when he considered the place home court advantage. Not that Callie needed it. But it eased some of the lingering tension in his muscles. Brought his paranoia level down to DEFCON two.

Calliope leaned against the wall, her mouth pursed tight and her hands fisted at her side. She'd been antsy since they'd left the hotel back in Puerto Rico, constantly checking her six despite the fact the threat should be over. But Booker had a bad feeling she wouldn't truly settle until Rogers had been convicted, and she could finally put the past year of her life to rest.

She glanced at him, smiled, then focused on her boss. "We tried. It just didn't work out that way."

"You tried? That's your official statement?"

"It's not like we had many options once those assholes in the car tried to kill us. After that…" She blew out a rough breath. "It was really just an exercise in damage control. A last-ditch effort to stay one step ahead."

Higgins ran his hand over his thinning hair. "You could have had Booker fly you anywhere other than that two-bit dirt road miles from that shack." He raised his brows. "In the middle of a storm."

"I think you know we…" She paused, staring at Higgins for a moment before shaking her head. "Couldn't, sir."

"Stubborn, as usual." He tapped the file on top of the table. "I'd like to go through everything one more time before we head back and make an official statement. Ensure I didn't miss anything. But, as I said in San Juan, it looks pretty cut and dry. If our IT guys can clean up the phone recording — maybe retrieve some audio from those wire taps — we should be able to keep Rogers in Leavenworth for the rest of his life. Which means, I owe you an apology, Callie. You were right. There was another mole."

She nodded, looking oddly uneasy. "I'm just glad he'll pay for what he did. That's all that matters."

"Agreed." Higgins nodded toward the hallway. "Why don't you two get some coffee and let me go through these files one more time? I won't be able to have it all wrapped up tonight, but I can quash any doubts that we've got a strong case — didn't leave anything important back in Puerto Rico. And you can work on your report so you can enjoy a couple of days off before you decide where you'd like to go next. Assuming this is as high profile as I expect it to be, you'll have your pick of assignments."

"I really just want to get some sleep. Spend a day without having to look over my shoulder."

Higgins chuckled. "Well, with any luck, you

shouldn't have any drug cartel waiting for you in the parking lot, tonight."

"That would be a nice change."

"One last thing." He tapped the folder, again. "You're sure you've given me everything. Neither you nor Booker are holding out on me, are you? Made copies I'm unaware of? Because we need the rest of this to be by-the-book after the way it went down."

Booker met her gaze, wondering if she'd tell her boss he'd sent Wyatt a copy of what he'd recorded on his phone along with all the photos they'd taken. Not that Booker was trying to break protocol, but after everything Callie had been through, he wasn't taking any chances all her evidence might be conveniently misplaced.

Calliope simply shook her head. "There wasn't time, so, you've got everything, sir."

Higgins looked at both of them, then nodded. "Okay. I'll text you as soon as I'm done." He snorted as they headed for the door. "You're just lucky Keith didn't know you'd come all the way to Montana to grab Booker, or he might have had someone cap you both outside that bar instead of waiting for you to get to Puerto Rico."

Callie nodded, then stopped, looking up at Booker before frowning. She twisted slightly, eyes narrowed. Mouth pinched tight. "How did you know about the bar... Shit!"

Booker inhaled, grabbing Callie and shoving her

through the doorway as the men beside Higgins drew their weapons — unloaded half a dozen rounds their way. They ricocheted off the frame, whizzing past them as Booker broke into a full sprint, pulling Callie with him.

She kept pace, rounding the corner then following him down the next corridor. Nearly crashing into Wyatt when the man came charging out of his computer lab. Gun drawn. Muscles primed for a fight.

He looked as if he might fire, then motioned for them to get behind him as he darted to the corner — peering out then firing a couple of cover rounds. "What the actual fuck, Booker?"

Booker shook his head, trying to catch his breath against the burning in his side. "No time for details, but Higgins is in on it, along with those assholes he brought with him. We need to disappear. Now."

Wyatt nodded, fired a few more shots, then he was up and running. Racing down the corridor — heading for the set of stairs at the end of the hallway. They got within a few feet of it when the lights blinked out. Brightly lit hallway one moment, nothing but eerie darkness the next.

Wyatt stopped, scanning the hallway. "Well, shit. The only way to take the power and backup systems completely offline is to hit the main control panel with an EM pulse device. And Higgins is definitely in the position to acquire one."

Wyatt motioned them to wait as he slipped through the emergency door, only to pop back out. "Half a dozen tangoes on the stairs. Run."

Booker turned, then took off. Down one of the shorter corridors then through a set of doors. What doubled as a suite if needed. He waited until Wyatt was through then twisted the dead bolt. Not that it would hold anyone off for long with the magnetic seal no longer working, but every second counted.

Callie was already trying the windows, nodding when she reached the last one. "What's that structure?"

Wyatt moved in beside her, half his focus still on the door. Gun at his side, but ready. "Hanger roof."

"It's not that far. I say we break the window then jump. Make more shit up as we go…" She looked back at him squinting before pointing at the floor. "Is that blood?"

She inhaled. "Christ, Booker, you're hit!"

"You're what?" Wyatt stepped toward him, but Booker waved them both off, pointing to the window.

"Shoot the damn window out. Worry about me, later. Or it won't matter because we'll all be dead."

Booker grunted when Callie knocked his hands away, then lifted his shirt. "It's not that bad. Let's just get on with this before those assholes bust down the door. Lock's not gonna hold them for long once they figure out where we went. And with me leaving a trail of blood down the damn hallway..."

"Not bad, my ass." She glared at him. "Half your shirt is soaked. Shit."

He took her hand. Smiled. "I'm fine. Been hurt worse. Ask Wyatt. He hasn't even had to carry my ass, yet. Now, are you shooting out the window, or am I?"

"You'll probably pass out if you tried to lift your damn arm that high. And put some pressure on that wound until we can get some help." She stepped back — fired. The glass cracked then shattered, spilling onto the floor in a sea of tiny squares.

But Wyatt was already moving, clearing away the bits still clinging to the frame, then looking out. "It's about ten feet. Not horrible, but..." He gave Booker the once-over. "Callie can go first. I'll sling you over my shoulder—"

"You're not slinging me over your shoulder. I can jump." He cursed when the door handle rattled. "We're out of time. Move."

Callie climbed onto the ledge, looking back at him. "I swear, if you fucking die on me..." Then she was disappearing into the night, the dull thud the only proof she'd made it.

Wyatt helped him up next, shaking his head when more blood pooled on the frame. "I second what she said. Don't fucking die."

Booker snorted, then jumped, screwing up the

landing when his legs buckled the moment he hit. He slid sideways, but Callie grabbed his jacket — managed to get him stopped and on his feet by the time Wyatt joined them.

His buddy didn't talk, just wrapped his arm around Booker's waist then started moving. Half-dragging Bookers' ass over to one of the skylights while Callie guarded their six. It only took a couple of hits to the break the glass. Then Wyatt was sweeping off the pieces and peering into the hanger.

Five seconds flat, and he was looking up. Pointing inside. "There's a moveable platform ladder off to the right. If we do this correctly, we should be able to land on it. But it's gonna hurt your side, buddy."

"Hurt I can live with." Booker cursed when shots sounded behind them. "And that's the door about to give way. Now would be a good time to jump."

Wyatt nodded, grabbed Booker then lowered him over the edge, releasing his wrists after swinging him sideways — dropping his ass onto the platform. He hit hard, but it beat falling the extra eight feet to the floor. What might have been the end of him moving under his own steam.

Callie landed like a freaking gazelle next to him, Wyatt bringing up the rear. Boots barely making a sound as he hit the metal, then swept the area, pausing at all the deeper shadows. Looking every inch the SEAL he'd always been.

Wyatt nodded at the doors. "Only a matter of

time before they're on us. And those doors aren't gonna hold them off long. Any ideas?"

Booker chuckled, stumbling his way down the metal steps. "Just one. But... you're not going to like it."

"Why wouldn't I... No."

Booker tripped off the bottom stair, nearly continuing to the floor before Callie caught him — shouldered most of his weight. "If you've got a better plan..."

"You're barely conscious."

"Not dead, yet. And we don't have to go far. Big Sky's only twenty minutes away. That should put enough distance between us and Higgins, and they can fix my side."

"That's assuming you don't bleed out on the way. And that's a pretty big if, buddy."

"I can make it." Booker held up his good hand. "Get the tie downs while I run through the checks. I'll need you to hit the automated doors once we're up and running, then get your ass in the seat because we both know those mercenaries are going to swarm the hanger the moment they've got an inch of room. Hell, Higgins might show up, too."

"Higgins I can handle. In fact, I'm in the zone. Might be better to chance it with the mercenaries..."

Booker gave Wyatt a shove, relying on Callie more than he wanted just to make his way to the helicopter and climb inside. It took two tries to actually get his legs to work — lift them enough to get over the frame — but he managed it. Thought he was going to puke, but he held it together. Got strapped in by the time Wyatt had cleared the area.

Not that Booker liked to fly without doing a thorough walk around, going through all the proper checks, but...

Having the hanger doors shake as shouts rose from the other side removed any doubts. Had Booker completely focused. He pushed in a number of circuit breakers, hoping the dials didn't immediately peg into the red, as he rolled on the throttle — got everything humming.

A series of thuds impacted the door from the other side. What was obviously Higgins' men trying to shoot their way in. A feat they might achieve if Booker didn't get them moving. Wyatt waited until Booker nodded, then hit the button, running back to the helicopter as Booker revved up the turbine. Cold to ready in record time, all the while praying the machine could handle the strain. Didn't overheat or start chucking out parts.

As expected, the assholes tried to breach the hanger the moment there were more than a few inches of space between the doors. Enough to get the muzzle in — start firing. Wyatt and Callie countered as best they could, keeping the main forces back until the space was too large and the men poured inside.

That was Booker's key to do his thing. While he

didn't want to risk using the helicopter as a weapon, like back in the clearing, he wasn't above scaring the shit out of the men. And if a few got hurt…

Two seconds in, and he had the chopper in a low hover, the downwash already knocking the creeps back. Another couple, and he got her spinning. Keeping everything within the confines of the walls — avoiding the other machine parked on the far side along with all the tools — while sending the men racing for cover. A few bullets ricocheted off the fuselage — one punching through the door by his feet — but the maneuver bought him the time they needed for the doors to open enough he could move out.

There was a moment of pause — of Wyatt and Callie yelling at him that they wouldn't fit — before he'd squeaked through. Was racing along the tarmac. Rain covering the bubble. A few forks of lightning flashing in the distance.

Higgins was off to the right, jumping into a black SUV. Booker didn't know if the bastard was making a run for it or calling in more forces. If he had a chopper on standby or a few more mercenaries with RPGs in the wings in case Callie got away.

Not that it mattered because Booker wasn't giving anyone a chance to target them, let alone shoot them down.

Wind howled through the cockpit as he lowered the machine, barely skimming over the ground.

Trees and brush passed in a blur, only those occasional bursts of lightning illuminating the landscape.

Wyatt keyed up the mike, glancing at him from the passenger side. "Buddy? I think we're good. You can gain a bit of altitude."

Booker huffed, shaking his head as a few dots started eating away at his peripheral vision. Fading the surroundings into muted shapes. "No way. I'm not taking the chance that asshole's got a chopper inbound. The lower we are, the less likely anyone is to see us."

"And the less likely you are to recover if something catastrophic happens."

"Emergencies, I can deal with. RPGs…"

Wyatt didn't comment, just tightened his harness, staring out the window as if it held the answers. Would give him the right words to convince Booker to ease up. Play it safe.

But he couldn't.

Wouldn't with Callie and Wyatt's lives hanging in the balance. If there was even a slight possibility this wasn't over…

Forty miles in, and he was still following the highway. Paralleling it in an effort to avoid anyone calling the state police. What could turn ugly before they had a chance to explain. Wyatt had wanted to call Stone, Gunnar — everyone. Get them to send backup. But Booker had refused. If Higgins hadn't rushed off, yet, the bastard might be able to track them using their radio broadcasts.

Wyatt had compromised and sent off a text. Told everyone to mobilize. That the facility had been infiltrated, and they were heading for Big Sky. Not that they knew if Stone or the others had received it. Between the storm and their positioning, it just kept spinning, trying to send.

Worries for later. After Booker had gotten them safely to the medical center because they were already pushing fifteen minutes, and he wasn't fairing that well. Those dots took up most of his useable vision. And whenever he tried to move his left arm… It sent a shooting pain into his chest. Made it hard to breathe. To keep his eyes open.

He went against the voices in his head and gained some altitude, hoping it might stabilize the scenery. But it only changed it from a light blur into a dark one. Everything still drifting into that numbing gray inside his head.

"Booker!"

He blinked, realized they were slightly nose down, then corrected, getting the chopper level, again.

Wyatt cursed, snapping his fingers in front of Booker's face. "You're scaring me, buddy. I called your name three times before you responded. You still with us?"

Booker glanced over at Wyatt, then motioned to

the controls. "Completely focused, but just in case... Remember that lesson I gave you?"

Wyatt snorted. "You mean that hour I spent shitting my pants? Yeah, I remember. Why?"

He paled when Booker simply stared at him. "No. No freaking way."

"Easy, Wyatt."

"Easy? I know that look, and there's no fucking way I'm flying this thing. Not in good weather, and definitely not at night in the middle of a storm."

"I don't need you to fly it just... Lend a hand."

"Lend a hand? What the hell does that even mean?"

"It means put your damn hands on the controls and keep it steady if I drift off for a second."

"Drift off?" Wyatt muttered under his breath, glancing back at Callie before fisting the controls. Looking as if he'd rather jump than touch the damn things. "I am so kicking your ass once we land."

"Callie might have something to say about that, seeing as she loves my sorry ass, but..." He coughed, sprayed a few flecks of blood across the bubble, before closing his eyes. Doing his best to shove it all down.

"Damn it, Booker, wake up!"

He jolted, nearly puked from the sudden shifting of the scenery, then glanced around. Alarms blared through the cockpit, several lights blinking on the dash.

He pulled back on the controls, narrowly missing a tree before gaining a bit of altitude. Holding on until the cabin went silent.

Wyatt grunted. "You're not going to stay conscious all the way to the hospital. We're close. Just put her down wherever you can, because in all my years as a SEAL, I've never thought I was going to die until two minutes, ago."

Booker nodded, scanning the landscape. Lights reflected in the distance, blurring from the rain across the glass. "There's nothing but trees and the highway between us and the clinic."

"Of course there isn't. Just, land on the highway if you need to, but don't crash into a truck."

"I'll do my best." He readied the chopper, slowly losing height, only to bank off to one side when a semi appeared out of some fog, horn blaring. Lights nearly blinding them. The truck whizzed past, water spraying off the top, before disappearing just as quickly. Nothing but utter blackness around them.

Callie leaned forward, pointing off to the right. "There. I'm pretty sure that's another road."

Booker nodded, lining up the cross road.

"Wires!"

Wyatt's voice boomed through the cockpit, as Booker tipped them back — climbing over the lines while swinging the gear to one side before leveling out. Centering them back on the road.

Wyatt followed him on the controls, keeping it

steady when Booker wasn't even convinced he was moving them, anymore. One hand slipped into his lap for a moment before he managed to grab the cyclic. Straighten them out.

Wyatt reached over — gave his shoulder a squeeze. "Just another minute, and you can rest all you want. I'll fucking run your ass to the hospital, just get us down in one piece."

His buddy made it sound so easy. As if staying awake was simple. Something Booker had done a thousand times. And he tried. Focused on keeping his eyes open, his hands moving. Watching the road inch closer, all that rain settling on the bubble. Distorting the view. But it all started fading. A series of streaks joining the dots across his vision. Voices sounded in the distance, hands grabbing his arms, as he gave it one last shot, hoping he'd actually landed, before his head fell forward, and everything went numb.

CHAPTER 15

HE WAS DEAD. And it was all her fault.

Calliope bolted from the chopper, yanking open Booker's door while everything was still rocking. The rotors whining overhead. Fumes whirling around her as thunder rolled across the sky, rain falling in steady sheets.

"Jesus." Blood. Everywhere. His shirt, the seat — pooling on the floor. "Booker? Baby, talk to me."

She gave him a shake when he didn't respond. "Wyatt? He needed a doctor twenty minutes, ago. God, how the hell did he stay conscious all this way?"

Wyatt rolled off the throttle, cranking some knobs under the seat before jumping out — meeting her on Booker's side. "Bastard's a piece of work. I'll take him. You run ahead and get them ready. He's gonna need all the blood they've got."

She nodded then took off, sprinting up the street.

Gun at the ready, just in case. God, how had she missed Higgins had teamed up with Rogers? It made so much sense, now. How Rogers had known she was in Puerto Rico. Why he hadn't been worried in the shack. How he'd known Booker was there. All clues she'd missed.

And Booker had paid the price.

Callie pushed the thoughts aside, pumping her arms harder. Picking up her feet just enough to gain a bit more speed. Wyatt wasn't that far behind, carrying Booker as if it was nothing. Looking tough and strong, each one of his strides matching two of hers.

She hit the sliding doors still sprinting, yelling out for a doctor. She pointed to the doors, badge in one hand, gun in the other. "I've got an agent incoming with a GSW to his right rib cage. Probably a forty-five. He's lost a ton of blood. He can't wait."

Some guy in scrubs frowned, then headed for the door, stepping back when Wyatt barreled through, blood covering half his shirt. He didn't speak just continued through the main section, down the hallway then into one of the trauma rooms, placing Booker on the stretcher, before turning and staring at the doctor. The kind of scowl Callie assumed got new recruits shitting their pants.

Wyatt leaned in close. "My best friend just saved our asses. You'd best save his."

It wasn't a threat. Not really. At least, not one

Callie thought would lead to anything. The vague kind she hoped the doctor would chalk up to emotions running high. But it got the man moving. Barking out orders as he did a quick once-over then hooked up an IV. Got a bag of O neg dripping into Booker's other arm.

Less than two minutes, and a full team was rushing around, grabbing supplies, writing down stats and numbers she didn't understand. Then, they were ushering her and Wyatt out, talking about how they needed room to do their job. That they couldn't transport Booker with the weather grounding the choppers and part of the road flooded. The shit-storm he'd flown in to ensure she and Wyatt were safe.

A slam of the door, and Booker was gone. Hidden behind the cold white door with nothing but a trail of blood as proof he'd been there. That she might lose the best thing to ever happen to her before she'd even had the chance to enjoy it.

To start the other half of the life she'd been waiting for.

A hand settled on her shoulder, and she turned into Wyatt, closing her eyes as he wrapped his arms around her. "He'll be okay. Booker's more stubborn than anyone I know. No way one tiny bullet's going to do him in."

She nodded, wanting to believe Wyatt was right. That, once Booker got a few pints of blood into him, he'd be fine. But the words wouldn't form on her tongue.

Wyatt sighed. "Come on. You need a once-over, too."

She shook her head, wrapping her arms around herself once she'd stepped back. "I'm fine. We need to call it in. Get the DEA's special ops team out to the site. Make sure there aren't a bunch of armed assholes hiding in the wings, waiting to ambush anyone who shows up. Get an ABP out on Higgins. Fuck, I can't believe I missed that."

"No one saw it coming. This isn't your fault."

"Tell that to Booker."

Wyatt moved over to her. "Booker will tell you, himself, once the bastard stops lazing around. In the meantime, let me see if I can raise Stone — get a proper sit rep. Then, we'll reassess. Though, you really should have a doctor look at your arms. You've got some cuts from the glass."

She glanced down, barely registering the lacerations along her forearms. "I'm fine. They can look at them after they've saved Booker."

"Calliope. I know you're scared, but Booker will have my ass when he wakes up if he discovers you sat here the entire time, bleeding, and I didn't do a damn thing about it."

"I'm not bleeding, anymore."

"Like that's gonna mean anything to Booker. The jerk's a bit overprotective, but he means well."

"Says the guy who jumped in front of us. Would have taken a bullet without question. You're both nuts, but... I guess that's part of your charm."

"It's an occupational hazard." He motioned toward a couple chairs pushed against the wall. "Come on. Standing here, obsessing over what we did or didn't do isn't going to help Booker. And if you're not going to let the doctors take a look at those injuries, then let's talk through what happened. Check in with Stone, and make sure your asshole boss doesn't get away with this. Okay?"

Callie glanced at the closed door, wishing she knew what was happening. Did they even have a surgical wing here? People who could save him? What if he needed a higher level of care? The quick look she'd taken of his side hadn't seemed that bad — what she'd guessed was a through-and-through — but she couldn't swear on it. Deduce if the damn bullet had hit any major organs on the way through.

God, what if he'd already died? If they'd decided he was beyond saving? Were just cleaning up all the blood. Calling out his time of death. What if she'd already lost him?

"Shit, Callie, you need to breathe for me."

Breathe? How could she breathe when Booker was dying beyond that stupid door? Bleeding out or having some kind of stroke?

Wyatt tsked, grabbed her head, then shoved it

between her knees. "Try not to think about anything. Just close your eyes. I'm right here."

Booker should be the one out here, stressing. Growling at his buddy, while she was lying on that stretcher. God, he needed to be okay.

Wyatt moved in close. He didn't ask her to talk, just shouldered up beside her, most likely waiting for her to pass out. So he could catch her before she'd given herself a concussion. It took a few minutes, and Wyatt bracing half her weight, but she finally got her lungs working. Managed not to completely break down.

"Better. Now, let's sit. I'll get that coffee, check in with Stone, and we'll talk once you're ready."

She nodded, thankful Wyatt hadn't commented on the tears streaming down her cheeks. How she was barely holding it together, despite the non-stop pep talk looping in her head. How Booker would be okay. How she'd find a way to make it up to him. Spend the rest of her life showing him they were worth this second chance.

Wyatt was back a few minutes later, paper cup in tow and what looked like a poor excuse for a muffin. He placed them on the table, holding out his phone. "I can't get any service, and the storm's taken out the landlines. The staff said we're lucky there's still power, so... Let's talk about Higgins until we can call in the cavalry, okay?"

She nodded, took a seat then started recapping

the meeting. What Higgins had said. How she'd finally figured out he was dirty. She was just getting to the part where she suspected Booker had gotten shot when the lights flickered then winked out. Nothing but the eerie glow of a distant exit sign illuminating the space.

Callie bolted to her feet, gun drawn, already scanning the darkness. "Shit."

Wyatt moved in beside her, Sig at his shoulder, head on a damn swivel. "It could just be from the storm."

"Right, because DEA douchebags don't kill the power when they send a wet squad after you. Besides, the backup generators would have kicked in, by now."

"There are a dozen places we could have gone. No way he figured it out, this quickly."

"Higgins has a nasty way of tracking… crap."

She reached into her pocket and removed the burner cell her boss had given her the previous week, before holding it up.

Wyatt huffed. "What's that?"

"The burner cell he gave me so he could *protect* me, the bastard. What do you want to bet he put some kind of GPS tracker inside it? And I watched the creep unbox it in his office. God, I'm a fool."

"It might not even be working after that trip down the river. This could be him guessing."

"Well, I'm sure the giant-ass chopper sitting on

the side of the highway let him know he'd guessed right."

"Glad you're as positive as Booker."

"I'm a fucking ray of sunshine." She motioned to the far end of the hall, quick-stepping down one side as Wyatt took the other. Nothing unusual sounded around them, the distant din of conversation still reaching them. Comments about how they'd have to check on the generators. That everyone should remain calm.

Wyatt counted to three once they'd reached the corner, both popping out to clear the adjoining hallways. Deep shadows pocketed the corridors, more exit signs glowing at the far ends.

Wyatt shifted over to her. "If they're here, they'll use a rear staff entrance. Avoid the main section, altogether. They'll travel in pairs if there're more than two, and attempt to keep casualties to a minimum, to avoid attracting more attention than necessary. They can spin us dying as just some double agents who probably turned on each other. If they kill a bunch of civilians…"

"Agreed. I'll go check it out. You stay here and make sure no one gets past me to Booker."

"Sorry, honey. We're a team. Period. I'll give the staff treating Booker a quick debrief — see if they can lock or barricade the door. But we go together. SEAL, remember. These assholes might think they've got the upper hand, but I guarantee they haven't done half the shit I have. And with you backing me up…"

He took off, heading for Booker's trauma room, and damn, the man didn't make a sound. Not a footfall, or a whisper of breath. Just him standing beside her one moment, disappearing into the shadows the next. Just like Booker had done in Puerto Rico. All that special training that made them unstoppable.

She'd thought about protesting. Insisting she take on Higgins or at least his men, alone. Prevent any further collateral damage, but she couldn't get the words out. Not when she knew Wyatt was far more skilled than her. Sure, she was an excellent shot, and she'd been in over a hundred raids, but that didn't quite meet SEAL level. And she wasn't too proud to say she wanted his help.

Needed it because this ended, here.

Wyatt was back in under a minute, shouldering up beside her. Calm. Focused. His breathing steady. Strong. Not that she was nervous, but her heart rate had definitely picked up a bit. A slight pounding in her chest that simply reminded her she had more than just her life to lose.

He motioned to the right, then followed after her, constantly checking their six, his pace matching hers. She did a quick check of each door they passed, either peeking inside or ensuring it was locked, then continued ahead. Gun sweeping the hallway with every step. Straining to hear anything out of the ordinary.

They made it down the length of the hall when a door whooshed somewhere up ahead. Likely down the distant corridor. The one fully encased in darkness with nothing but even deeper pockets of shadows lining it. What she thought led to the staff parking at the rear, just like Wyatt had suggested.

Wyatt obviously heard it, too, because he was up and in front of her a second later, keeping her back as he darted to the corner, showed the countdown on his hand the darted out. Up and over to a small alcove partway down the hall. Not much cover, but some.

Callie covered him until he'd gained another ten feet before following his path, using the alcove then darting in the doorway across from him. He made a few signals with his hands. He'd stay left, she'd go right, and they'd meet at the next corner.

Spotting a laser sight bounce off the wall next to Wyatt the moment she stepped out made her change her mind. Had her lunging at him, knocking him back a second before the wall exploded, bits of drywall spraying across the floor.

Wyatt rolled with the impact, regaining his feet, then yanking her up and shoving her into a doorway a moment later. Crowding her over as he wedged himself in front. What she assumed was his way of blocking any shot. Ensuring he'd be the one to take a hit.

Screw that.

"I don't need a shield. Go! Before they flank or relay we're on to them if they've got backup."

And she knew as sure as this conflict would end bloody, there were more. Four, maybe six, total. However many Higgins had managed to fit in his over-sized SUV.

The only wildcard was whether Higgins was part of the team. While, he hadn't been in the field in years, this was personal, and she had a feeling he'd want to make a stand. Maybe try to bargain with her, like Keith had.

Wyatt glanced back at her, eyes narrowed. A hint of color high on his cheekbones. "I swear to god if you die on me…"

"Feeling's mutual, jackass. Go. I've got your six."

Another second of him staring at her, then he was out and running, firing off a couple rounds when one of the men tried to dart out of the shadows — catch them before they reached the corner.

One shot, and the perp was down. No rolling or staggering just the retort of Wyatt's gun, and the guy was on the ground. Motionless. His partner fired up the hallway, using way more rounds than necessary, but Wyatt was already squished into a doorway, waiting until the asshole paused before capping him, too. A damn one-man wet squad without the body armor or night vision goggles.

She moved out to join him when a footstep sounded behind her. Callie had just enough time to dive — get to the corner before the hallway lit up. A steady stream of bullets ricocheting off the doors, the walls. What she assumed was the asshole's attempt at killing them without aiming.

A stray round caught her in the thigh — carving a groove along her skin as it took an odd bounce off a door — embedding into the wall behind her. Pain burned down her leg, but she managed to cross over to Wyatt without getting hit, again. Scoot in behind him.

He looked at her leg, frowned, then returned fire. "You good?"

She nodded, hissing out her next breath. "It hurts like a bitch, but it's just a graze. We need to split up. I'll go left, see how many I can draw down to the imagining department while you take care of any threats in the parking lot. Maybe hiding outside."

"And leave you alone? I don't think so."

"Wyatt. We both know we need to get some fire-power in behind them. I'll be okay. You're the one who's taking the real risk. There could be a dozen men outside. I doubt more than a couple will follow me. They know you're the threat, and they'll adjust accordingly."

"I can handle however many they send."

"Good, then go thin the herd. I'll be buying a bit of time in X-ray or the MRI."

"Calliope..."

"I promise. I won't take any unnecessary risks. And, once you're done with the rest of them, you can circle back — bust in and save the day. Deal?"

He grunted as if it hurt. Probably because he knew she was right. They'd never come out ahead if they didn't gain the upper hand. Find a way to outflank them. And Wyatt was their best shot.

He gave her a curt nod followed by one of his death glares, then was up and running. Down the corridor, eliminating another tango before Wyatt was through the far exit doors and out of sight. Ten seconds flat.

More bullets followed in his wake, and she used the temporary distraction to hoof it down the corridor, around the corner then through the doors and into the imagining department. What she hoped would be enough cover to give her the advantage — take them out one at a time.

Footsteps shadowed her move, slowing once they reached the doors. There were a few moments of eerie silence, then the door opening. Not much, just an inch or two. Enough to peek inside — get a bead on her location.

Callie didn't move — didn't breathe — waiting until the guy was inside and heading for the far wall before she fired. Dropped him with a shot to the head.

Another guy barreled through a second later, diving across the room then spinning toward her. He didn't aim, just started firing, bullets pinging off the machines. She wedged herself behind the X-Ray machine, counted to three then popped up and fired. Missed a bit wide the first time but caught his leg the next. It wasn't fatal but it knocked him back — gave her enough time to fire, again. Hit him in the shoulder just outside his armor.

The guy slammed against the wall, leaving a bloody smear along the paint as he slid to the floor, rifle clattering to the linoleum.

She moved, darting across the room, managing to squeeze behind a trolly when the door opened, again, a lone shadow just visible on the floor.

"I have to say, Calliope, I'm impressed. If I'd known you were this hard to kill, I might have risked trying earlier. Before you got your friends involved."

Higgins. And the bastard was gloating. As if he'd known all along it would come down to him and her.

Calliope chanced a quick look, ducking back as he fired her way, bouncing the round off the metal table. "Trust me, Higgins, the feeling's mutual. I could have capped you in Puerto Rico and just been done with it."

"I was actually surprised you didn't. That it took you so long to figure out I'd been playing you.

Tracking you the entire time, though, I suppose discovering Keith was involved probably knocked you for a loop. Mentor and all that."

"Don't worry. I know exactly who I can trust, now. So, thanks for that."

"Yes, Booker and his crew. I'll admit, I didn't see that coming. Hadn't realized you two were so close until everything went down in San Juan. That's why I didn't attempt anything before we returned. Your circle of friends is just a bit too good. Which brings us to now. Give me the evidence I know Booker copied, and I'll leave. Let everything fall out as it needs to."

She snorted, chancing a quick scoot to the MRI, diving in behind it just as Higgins fired. Nearly caught her in the shoulder. "Those bullets you keep firing suggest you're lying."

"Stop running, and I'll stop firing. I just want those copies."

She shifted around to the back. What might be her one chance to get behind him. "If that was true, you would have asked, instead of bringing a wet squad with you."

"Letting you live isn't my main objective. I'm just giving you a choice to speed things along. I'll count to ten, then, I'll just have one of my guys blow the room. The entire hospital, if needed. Gas lines can be such a bitch. One…"

He was serious. He'd have one of those assholes

toss in a grenade or flash bang inside. Maybe set a charge on the equipment or hold true to his threat and blow the entire center.

The fact none of his men had joined him, yet, was encouraging. Proof that Wyatt was working his way through their ranks. Eliminating the other threats. Which just left Higgins.

"I can only imagine what's in the photos we took that's got you worked up enough you'd follow us here instead of making a run for the border. Guess I should have scrutinized them before leaving Puerto Rico, but then, I thought I could trust you."

"We all make mistakes, Jensen. I'm at five, are you stepping out or am I creating a tragic incident?"

She snorted, removing her burner, then shuffling around to the far side of the unit, before darting to another table of instruments several feet away. Praying she didn't make enough noise he'd notice. Popping up without him opening fire was one of the few times she'd been surprised in a good way.

Higgins huffed. "Guess we'll do this the hard way. Just remember. I gave you the choice. All these people didn't have to die."

Callie took a breath, ran through her plan then stood, tossing the phone at his feet. "Dodge that, asshole."

The cell skipped along the floor, each impact echoing through the room. Higgins inhaled, then dove for cover, shielding his head for a few moments

— obviously expecting something to explode. But Callie was already up and running, half her focus on the door in case one of his agents appeared out of the shadows, then stopped with her gun aimed at Higgins' head. No way for him to dodge or counter before she got off a shot.

He cursed, then stood. "Not bad. I really thought you had a grenade."

"I want to see your hands, or I'll just drop you."

"I don't think so."

He raised his arm, only to jerk backwards, slamming against one of the tables before crumpling to the floor. Blood staining his shoulder. Each labored breath sounding like it might be his last.

She moved over to him, kicking his gun away when the doors whooshed open, a huge silhouette filling the opening.

Callie turned, aimed, then grunted, shaking her head. "God damn it, Wyatt. I nearly shot you."

Wyatt stepped forward, still scanning the room before closing the distance. "I thought you might be dead. Christ, don't scare me like that, again."

"Says the guy who took on how many tangoes?"

Wyatt merely shrugged. "He still breathing?"

"Barely."

"Shame." He waved his fingers at her. "They're evacuating the building. I caught one of his assholes rigging the gas main. I can't guarantee there isn't another device, so…"

"What about Higgins?"

"I suppose I can carry his ass, if you really want to save him."

"Wyatt…"

"Fine. Be all noble." He bent over then hoisted the man up. "Get the lead out, honey."

"What about Booker?"

"Semi-conscious and already bitching. He's in an ambulance outside." He started jogging. "Seriously, Calliope. Move, now, chat later."

Callie followed him out, trying not to limp too much until they were clear of any possible blast zone — had made their way to Booker's ambulance. Wyatt tossed Higgins on a stretcher, talking to the staff as she climbed inside, stopping cold, because… he was there. Alive. Looking far too pale, with blood still caked on his chest, but breathing.

She stumbled over to him, smiling when he blinked, taking a moment to focus before inhaling. Reaching for her hand.

He grimaced at what she assumed were his stitches pulling on his skin, gently placing their joined hands in his lap. "You're crazy."

She laughed, might have cried a bit, smiling at him as she leaned forward. Drank him in. "About you? Definitely."

"You took on another wet squad?"

"Wyatt took on the wet squad. I just dealt with the leftovers. He's very greedy, by the way."

"Calliope…"

"Shut up, and let me kiss you."

He rolled his eyes, then lifted his hand and speared it through her hair. She wanted to tell him to stop — that it was too soon to be moving that side — but the kiss was too sweet. Too damn hot to argue about. It wasn't until Wyatt cleared his throat that she pulled back and glanced over her shoulder.

The guy groaned. "Get a room."

Booker relaxed against the stretcher, eyeing his buddy. "Technically, this is my room, so… You might want to step out before we really get busy."

"You're not doing anything for a while. I know. I talked to the doctor. Besides, your girlfriend needs her leg treated, before she takes a page from your playbook and passes out."

"Her leg?" Booker groaned, but managed to shift forward enough he got a look at her thigh. "Is that a gunshot wound?"

Callie waved it off. "*You* had a gunshot wound. This is just a scrape."

"A scrape from a bullet *is* a gunshot wound. Shit. Wyatt, get the doctor, get—"

She kissed him, again, grinning at Wyatt when the man made retching noises then went to find a doctor. "I'm fine, Booker. Really. And, it's over."

Booker scoffed. "I doubt both of those."

"How about, it's over, for now."

"And your leg?"

"Burns like a son of a bitch, but at least I'm not insisting on flying a helicopter for twenty minutes."

"Life and death, sweetheart. And your life trumps everything."

She leaned in, again, drawing her finger along his chest. "I hope you mean that, baby, because I have big plans once you're back on your feet. And I intend on seeing them through."

Booker smiled, his eyes already drifting closed. "I'll be sure to get a doctor's note. Now, scoot your ass on here until Wyatt brings back a doctor. And no arguing. We'll get a double stretcher."

"Deal. I still love your sorry ass, by the way."

"Amazing ass, and I love yours more. Now, shut up and hold me."

CHAPTER 16

Booker stood in the doorway, watching Callie stare at the setting sun, the orange hue coloring her skin a brilliant gold. She'd been doing that every night since they'd finally been released from the medical center and shuttled back home. Stone had insisted they stay in a cabin on a fellow Brotherhood Protector's ranch until everyone was confident they weren't in further danger. That no one else in the DEA was going to send a wet squad after them.

Or maybe the cartel from Puerto Rico seeking revenge.

The change in scenery had put a lot of things into perspective for Booker, especially where Calliope was concerned. And with September only a couple of days away, he needed to get it all out in the open.

Her phone rang, and she sighed, checking the ID before silencing it. Shoving it back in her pocket.

Booker tsked, smiling at her when she turned to look at him, all ruby red lips and bright blue eyes. "You know, sweetheart, you'll have to talk to DC sooner or later."

Callie shrugged, focusing back on the sunset. "They can wait. I don't want to miss when it turns to purple."

He moved in behind her, wrapping his arms around her waist. His side tugged a bit, but he ignored it. He'd been extremely lucky. The bullet had glanced off a rib, cracked another then made its way back out. Other than a bit of shrapnel they'd had to dig out, he'd come through fairly unscathed. The biggest hurdle had been weakness due to blood loss.

Callie snuggled into him, and everything clicked into place. Like a lock turning over. And he knew he'd do whatever it took to spend every night just like this one. Calliope in his arms. The world slowly passing them by. "Does this pull on your ribs?"

He nipped at the soft spot behind her ear. "What ribs?"

"Jackass."

"I definitely prefer baby. Jackass makes me think you're dreaming of Wyatt."

She laughed. Deep. Genuine. "The guy's impressive, I'll grant you that. The way he took out all those men…"

She sighed, and Booker knew she wasn't concentrating on them, anymore. That the pressure of

235

deciding if she was going to accept the DEA's offer was still eating at her soul. He just wasn't sure if it was because she didn't want to accept it, or because she did.

He took a breath, ran over the speech in his head, then groaned when a truck turned onto the gravel road, the tires spitting out rocks as it bounced along.

Callie glanced over his shoulder, grinning. "It's like they know I was just about to take advantage of your weakened state."

Booker tapped her on the ass. "The only thing that's weak is your sense of humor."

She stuck her tongue out at him then walked down the path, greeting his crew as they scrambled out of Wyatt's truck. There were a few cat calls about how the two of them needed to stop screwing on the porch, before they headed inside. Unloaded all the takeout.

Wyatt handed him a plate, thanking Callie when she handed him a Coke instead of a beer. "So, you finally ready to get your ass back to work? Or are you going to laze around for another couple of weeks?"

Booker held up one hand. "I was ready to come back the next day, but you were all antsy about me flying around half-baked on pain meds."

"You thought you had wings. Trust me, no one wanted you behind the controls."

Callie stepped up to him and gave his ass a tap,

this time. "I don't know. I think if anyone could fly, it's you, baby."

That got him another round of groans and razzing. The guys all calling him *baby* for the rest of the night, while batting their eyes. Making kissing faces. Callie merely grinned the whole time, looking sexy and hot and so damn beautiful it made his chest ache. Right where the bullet would have killed him if he'd been one second slower at clearing the room.

His buddies stayed until he'd lost a hundred bucks at poker, then filed out, still laughing. Shoving each other as they argued about who got to ride shotgun. Wyatt lingered behind, toeing the wooden floorboards on the porch until Booker finally gave the man a punch to his arm.

He leaned against the post, eyeing his friend. "Just spit it out."

Wyatt crossed his arms over his chest. "Spit what out?"

"Whatever you've been wanting to say all night but had to wait until the rest of the guys were out of earshot."

"That obvious?"

"Please, how long have we known each other?"

Wyatt chuckled. "Too long if you ever make me fly a chopper, again."

"You did great. But that's not what you wanted to say, so… Just spit it out."

His buddy looked over his shoulder, glancing inside the house.

Booker sighed. "Calliope's in the bathroom getting ready for bed. She acts all tough, but the past few weeks have really taken a toll. Hell, the past year's taken a toll. It's just us, so…"

"I know a guy who works in the DEA. His brother's a SEAL. We did a few missions together. Anyway, with all the stonewalling you've been getting about what was in that evidence that was worth Higgins following us all the way to Big Sky instead of hopping a flight to Mexico, I asked him to discretely dig around."

Well shit.

"And?"

Wyatt checked the doorway, again. "He didn't have any names, but it's bad. There's talk it involves some bigwig in DC. That it might take years to unravel exactly who's involved." Wyatt took a step back. "I just wanted to let you know. I get Callie's a brilliant agent, but… I just don't know how safe it's going to be for her."

"Not safe at all, if my guess is right."

Booker cursed under his breath, spinning to see Calliope standing just inside the door, his shirt hanging down to her knees, her hair pinned up in some kind of messy bun.

Wyatt snorted, swatting Booker across the shoulder. "In the bathroom, my ass." He nodded at Callie.

"I wasn't trying to hide anything from you, I just didn't want to upset you. I know this has to be a hard pill to swallow."

She shrugged, but Booker didn't miss how the small smile she flashed them didn't reach her eyes. She'd been faking it ever since they'd come back from Puerto Rico, and he knew it was eating at her. "I knew there'd be fallout. Just not sure how much, yet."

"Let me know if you want my buddy to dig a bit deeper. Bastard's brother owes me so..."

"I'm sure DC will be perfectly vague the next time we chat."

Wyatt glanced at Booker, then said goodnight, yelling at the guys to stop playing all that eighties crap before jumping in his truck — driving off. Booker watched the taillights fade before heading inside and making his way to the bedroom. She was standing by the window, gazing out across the fields, looking so lost he had to physically stop himself from rushing over and asking her how to fix everything.

Especially when he knew he couldn't fix it. That it was something she had to come to terms with on her own. All he could do was be there to help her pick up the pieces. Put them back together in a way he hoped would include him in her life.

Her phone rang, again, and she let her head bow forward before she silenced it, then tossed it on the chair.

Booker walked over to her, taking her in his arms.

Hoping she didn't pull away. Having her lean against him eased the jumpy feeling in his gut. And he knew, no matter the cost, they'd find a way to make them work.

Callie hummed when he kissed her neck, tilting her head to the side in order to grant him better access. "I hope this is the start to some mind-blowing sex because I've been wet since we got back, and there hasn't been a damn thing I could do about it."

"Are you saying I haven't kept you satisfied?"

"You were kind of busy dying on me."

"I was never going to die. And I believe we've been humping like bunnies for the past week."

"Not enough. I need more."

"I'll make you a deal. You tell me why you keep ghosting your new boss, and I'll make you scream for the next two hours."

She looked back at him. "Two hours?"

"Two hours… *If* you tell me why you keep ignoring your phone. I know it's DC calling."

She slipped out of his arms, pacing across the room before spinning and bridging her weight on the far wall. "DC can wait."

"They've been waiting for three weeks. You can't stall them forever."

"I've still got two more days on my mandatory medical leave. They can wait."

"Calliope." He ambled over, getting close but not

touching her. "Talk to me. What's going through that amazing head of yours?"

"Nothing."

"Sweetheart. It's okay. I know they want you to head the investigation in DC. Probably take over a supervisory role at one of their district offices. And if that's what you want to do, then just tell me. We can find a way to make it work."

She leaned her head back, watching him through lowered lashes. "You'd do that? Either travel or consider moving? Leaving Wyatt and your brothers behind, because that's what this is, right? A brotherhood?"

He inched closer, tucking some lose strands behind her ear. "Do I want to leave? No. Would I if that was what it took for us to be together? Hell, yes. I'm not saying it would be easy, but… I love you. That trumps everything else."

Shit. Tears. Pooling in her eyes then slipping down her cheeks. Falling to the floor like tiny shards of glass. He opened his mouth to apologize. To say something — anything to stop her from crying — when she grabbed him by the shirt and tugged him against her, that soft, velvety mouth crushing over his.

Booker threaded his fingers through her hair, pulling her impossibly closer as he swallowed her needy cries, nipping his way down her neck then back up, eating at her mouth, again. He wasn't sure how much time passed before he was finally ready to ease back. Suck in some air.

Callie stayed close, her lips kiss-swollen. Those gorgeous eyes all dark and lust blown. She brushed her mouth over his, smiling at his raspy breath. "Booker."

"I mean it. I love you, Calliope. So, unless you're trying to tell me you don't want a future together, I'll—"

"I quit."

"Do whatever it…" He stopped, giving his head a shake because he swore she'd just said she'd quit. "You what?"

God, her smile. It was like that sunset from earlier all golden and warm. "I said, I quit. That's why DC keeps calling me. I told them to take their job and… well, you know."

He blinked, staring at her, the words still processing inside his head. "You… quit?"

"Did you get a concussion I'm unaware of, or are you just going deaf in your advanced age?"

"I'm only five years older than you, and I'm asking because I'm… Fuck, I'm speechless. Are you okay with this? Did I pressure you? Are you happy—"

She silenced him with a finger across his mouth. "So many questions. Yes, I'm okay with this. No, you didn't pressure me, and as long as I have you… I'm perfect. I love your sorry ass, remember? And there's nothing I want more than to show you just how much for the next sixty years."

"Hell, yeah, you do." He brushed his knuckles along her cheek. "So, would now be a good time to ask you to move in with me? And tell you that I want to buy a place of our own, just like this. With a bit of land and a whole lot of rooms to fill up?"

More tears, but he didn't freak out.

She nuzzled his nose. "Now would be the perfect time to ask. But before you go thinking that I'm hanging everything up, this is just a change in vocation. In fact, I was thinking we could get a place that has a small office attached to it. So I don't have to commute to work."

"Commute to work? What are you going to do?"

"Start my own private investigation company, of course. I mean, who better to unearth a bunch of secrets than a former agent?" She drew her finger along his chest like she did whenever she was trying to seduce him. "Just imagine the things I can uncover."

Booker tugged her hard against him. "A PI, huh? I like the sound of that. As long as you promise not to spy on me."

"You got something to hide, baby?"

He ground his erection against her stomach. "Just this."

"That seems serious. I think I should take a closer look."

"That might be dangerous."

"I'm counting on it. Now, how about you put all that healing to good use and carry me to bed. I have a new mission for you, and it's going to take all night."

Team EAGLE
Booker's Mission - Kris Norris
Hunter's Mission - Kendall Talbot
Gunn's Mission - Delilah Devlin
Xavier's Mission - Lori Matthews
Wyatt's Mission - Jen Talty

OTHER BOOKS BY KRIS NORRIS

SINGLES

CENTERFOLD

KEEPING FAITH

IRON WILL

MY SOUL TO KEEP

RICOCHET

ROPE'S END

SERIES

'TIL DEATH

1 - DEADLY VISION

2 - DEADLY OBSESSION

3 - DEADLY DECEPTION

BROTHERHOOD PROTECTORS ~ Elle James

1 - MIDNIGHT RANGER

2 – CARVED IN ICE

3 - GOING IN BLIND

4 - DELTA FORCE: COLT

5 - DELTA FORCE: CROW

6 - DELTA FORCE: PHOENIX

TEAM EAGLE

1 - BOOKER'S MISSION

TEAM FALCO

FIGHTING FOR FIONA

TEAM RAPTOR

LOGAN'S PROMISE

COLLATERAL DAMAGE

1 - FORCE OF NATURE

DARK PROPHECY

1 - SACRED TALISMAN

2 - TWICE BITTEN

3 - BLOOD OF THE WOLF

ENCHANTED LOVERS

1 - HEALING HANDS

FROM GRACE

1 - GABRIEL

2 – MICHAEL

THRESHOLD

1 - GRAVE MEASURES

TOMBSTONE

1 - Marshal Law

2 - Forgotten

3 - Last Stand

WAYWARD SOULS

1 - Delta Force: Cannon

2 - Delta Force: Colt

3 - Delta Force: Six

4 - Delta Force: Crow

5 - Delta Force: Phoenix

COLLECTIONS

Blue Collar Collection

Dark Prophecy: Vol 1

Into the Spirit, Boxed Set

COMING SOON

Delta Force: Priest

Team Watchdog — Ryder's Watch

ABOUT KRIS NORRIS

Author, single mother, slave to chaos—she's a jack-of-all-trades who's constantly looking for her ever elusive clone.

Kris loves connecting with fellow book enthusiasts. You can find her on these social media platforms...

krisnorris.ca
contactme@krisnorris.ca

f facebook.com/kris.norris.731
o instagram.com/girlnovelist
a amazon.com/author/krisnorris

BROTHERHOOD PROTECTORS

ORIGINAL SERIES BY ELLE JAMES

Bayou Brotherhood Protectors

Remy (#1)

Gerard (#2)

Lucas (#3)

Beau (#4)

Rafael (#5)

Valentin (#6)

Landry (#7)

Simon (#8)

Maurice (#9)

Jacques (#10)

Brotherhood Protectors Yellowstone

Saving Kyla (#1)

Saving Chelsea (#2)

Saving Amanda (#3)

Saving Liliana (#4)

Saving Breely (#5)

Saving Savvie (#6)

Saving Jenna (#7)

Saving Peyton (#8)

Brotherhood Protectors Colorado

SEAL Salvation (#1)

Rocky Mountain Rescue (#2)

Ranger Redemption (#3)

Tactical Takeover (#4)

Colorado Conspiracy (#5)

Rocky Mountain Madness (#6)

Free Fall (#7)

Colorado Cold Case (#8)

Fool's Folly (#9)

Colorado Free Rein (#10)

Rocky Mountain Venom (#11)

High Country Hero (#12)

Brotherhood Protectors

Montana SEAL (#1)

Bride Protector SEAL (#2)

Montana D-Force (#3)

Cowboy D-Force (#4)

Montana Ranger (#5)

Montana Dog Soldier (#6)

Montana SEAL Daddy (#7)

Montana Ranger's Wedding Vow (#8)

Montana SEAL Undercover Daddy (#9)

Cape Cod SEAL Rescue (#10)

Montana SEAL Friendly Fire (#11)

Montana SEAL's Mail-Order Bride (#12)

SEAL Justice (#13)

Ranger Creed (#14)

Delta Force Rescue (#15)

Dog Days of Christmas (#16)

Montana Rescue (#17)

Montana Ranger Returns (#18)

Hot SEAL Salty Dog (SEALs in Paradise)

Hot SEAL,Hawaiian Nights (SEALs in Paradise)

Hot SEAL Bachelor Party (SEALs in Paradise)

Hot SEAL, Independence Day (SEALs in Paradise)

Brotherhood Protectors Boxed Set 1

Brotherhood Protectors Boxed Set 2

Brotherhood Protectors Boxed Set 3

Brotherhood Protectors Boxed Set 4

Brotherhood Protectors Boxed Set 5

Brotherhood Protectors Boxed Set 6

ABOUT ELLE JAMES

ELLE JAMES also writing as MYLA JACKSON is a *New York Times* and *USA Today* Bestselling author of books including cowboys, intrigues and paranormal adventures that keep her readers on the edges of their seats. When she's not at her computer, she's traveling, snow skiing, boating, or riding her ATV, dreaming up new stories. Learn more about Elle James at www.ellejames.com

Website | Facebook | Twitter | GoodReads | Newsletter | BookBub | Amazon

Or visit her alter ego Myla Jackson at mylajackson.com
Website | Facebook | Twitter | Newsletter

Follow Me!
www.ellejames.com
ellejamesauthor@gmail.com